THE LONG SEARCH

When Deputy Sheriff Cliff McLaine was brutally tortured and murdered by the notorious gang of outlaws led by Will Jordan, his lawman brother Brad McLaine quit his job to embark on a search for the killers. His pursuit took him to New Mexico Territory, to Texas and to the Indian Territory where the Jordan gang had gone into hiding. But would Brad's grit, tenacity and gun-handling experience be enough to bring a ruthless band of outlaws to justice?

ALAN IRWIN

THE LONG SEARCH

Complete and Unabridged

LINFORD
Leicester

First published in Great Britain in 2006 by
Robert Hale Limited
London

First Linford Edition
published 2007
by arrangement with
Robert Hale Limited
London

LP

1765781

Irwin, Alan, 1916 –
    The long search.—Large print ed.—
Linford western library
1. Western stories
2. Large type books
I. Title
823.9'14 [F]

ISBN 978–1–84617–624–1

Published by
F. A. Thorpe (Publishing)
Anstey, Leicestershire

Set by Words & Graphics Ltd.
Anstey, Leicestershire
Printed and bound in Great Britain by
T. J. International Ltd., Padstow, Cornwall

1

As Brad McLaine rode from the north into the small town of Rogan, in the north-east corner of New Mexico Territory, he was conscious that the three men standing on the boardwalk outside the saloon were regarding him with interest. The time was five minutes before noon.

Brad was pretty sure from their dress and appearance that they were not townspeople. There was a faintly hostile look about them, and each of them was wearing a six-gun in a right-hand holster.

He headed for the livery stable further along the street, on the same side as the saloon. From the sign over the door he could see that the owner was Cal Turner. As Brad dismounted outside the stable door Turner came out.

'Howdy,' he said. He was a stocky man in his early forties who, three years previously, had arrived in Rogan with his wife to set up in business as a liveryman. He was normally a cheerful man but his customary smile was absent on that particular morning. He looked as though there was something on his mind.

'Howdy,' Brad replied. 'I'm aiming to stay the night here. Can you take care of my horse? We've covered a good many miles today.'

Turner hesitated a moment before replying, while he took a good look at Brad. He saw a tallish man in his late twenties, well-built, and carrying a Colt .45 Peacemaker in a right-hand holster. He was wearing a smart Texas hat. Turner sensed that here was a man well able to take care of himself.

'Sure, I can take care of your horse,' he said, 'but I know that all the rooms at the hotel are taken. And what's more I think you'd be doing yourself a favour if you dropped the idea of staying over

2

here, and rode right out of town.'

Surprised, Brad looked at the livery-man.

'You got a good reason for saying what you just did?' he asked.

'I sure have,' Turner replied. 'You saw the three men standing outside the saloon when you rode in?'

'I did,' Brad replied. 'They didn't look like the sort of men you'd expect to see in a small town like this. I figured maybe they were just passing through.'

'No such luck,' said Turner. 'They rode in two days ago and said they were staying in town for a while. Said they were expecting free food and accommodation and liquor for themselves, and free stabling for their horses.

'Otherwise, they said, they would shoot the town up and somebody was liable to get hurt. There's nobody here to stand up to them, so we've just had to give them what they wanted. I don't know when they're figuring to leave.

'If they start bothering you it'll be a case of three against one. That's why I suggested it might be a good idea for you to move on right now.'

'You got any idea who they are?' asked Brad.

'Myself, I ain't seen them before,' replied the liveryman, 'but Seth Binney, the storekeeper, saw them once in Pueblo in Colorado when he was visiting friends there. One of them's called Brett Jordan. He's the leader. The other two are called Dawson and Purdy. The word in Pueblo was that they were involved in a couple of stagecoach robberies, but there was no clear evidence against them.'

Brad, who had started on hearing the name Brett Jordan, spoke.

'Would you happen to know,' he asked, 'whether Brett Jordan is related to the outlaw Will Jordan? I heard a rumour that Will had a younger brother.'

'That's right,' said the liveryman. 'According to Seth Binney, Brett and Will Jordan are brothers. Seems they don't ride together, but all the same they're very close.'

Looking along the street towards the saloon, Turner saw his wife come out of the general store and start walking along the boardwalk towards him. She was an attractive woman, a few years younger than himself, who had provided invaluable help to him in setting up the livery stable.

As Turner watched his wife she came abreast of the saloon, outside which Jordan and his two companions were still standing. Jordan said something to the others; all three laughed and moved across to stand in the woman's path. She swerved to avoid them, but they moved sideways to block her way once again.

She stood still, looking angrily at the three grinning men standing in front of her. She suspected that they had been drinking in the saloon.

As Turner suddenly stiffened, Brad followed his eyes along the street.

'Damn Jordan and his men!' said the liveryman. 'That's my wife they're bothering.'

He started walking quickly along the street towards the saloon. Brad dropped the reins of his horse and followed the liveryman, a few paces behind. As Turner drew close to the saloon he stepped down on to the street, then walked on until he was abreast of the three men. He called out to them.

'Leave my wife be,' he said. 'Let her pass.'

Jordan and his companions turned their heads to look at the liveryman standing, unarmed, on the street below them. As they did so Brad moved up to stand by Turner's side and Martha Turner stepped down on to the street. She ran to join her husband and Brad. The three men on the boardwalk turned, and stood looking down at Brad and the Turners.

'That's a mighty good-looking woman you've got there, liveryman,' said Jordan, grinning. 'You can't blame us for wanting to get better acquainted.'

'She wants nothing to do with the likes of you,' said Turner. 'Leave her alone.'

Jordan's grin faded. 'Maybe we'll pay you a call at the livery stable later,' he said. 'We do what we like in this town.'

'Maybe that can be changed,' said Brad, who had moved a little further along the street, away from the Turners. 'It don't seem right to me that bullies like you should reckon they have the right to take a small town over and pester the womenfolk.'

The three men standing side by side on the boardwalk stared angrily at Brad.

'You reckon to do something about it?' asked Jordan.

'Not if you three leave town right now,' Brad replied. 'You sure ain't welcome here.'

Jordan flushed with anger. 'You asked for it,' he said, and went for his gun, confident, as were his two companions, that his well-known gun-handling ability would rid them of this meddlesome stranger.

But he had met his master. With eye-defeating rapidity, which greatly impressed the small group of onlookers, Brad pulled his long-barrelled Peace-maker smoothly from its holster, cocked it, and lined it up on Jordan's chest. The bullet from his gun drilled into his opponent's body before Jordan was ready to fire.

Jordan collapsed on the boardwalk. Purdy went for his gun, and Brad, with time to shoot only to wound, sent a bullet into his right arm, just above the elbow. Purdy dropped his gun without firing.

Belatedly, Dawson made a move for his gun, then stopped abruptly as he saw that Brad's cocked gun was pointing directly at him. He raised his hands to shoulder-height as Brad stepped up on to the boardwalk and relieved him of his revolver. Brad then collected the weapons of Purdy and Jordan, and threw all three six-guns on to the boardwalk well out of reach. Keeping the two men covered, he bent down over the man lying on the boardwalk. Jordan, shot through the heart, was clearly dead. Brad straightened up, and spoke to the two men standing in front of him.

'What I want you two to do,' he said, 'is to settle for everything you've taken here without payment. Then I want you to leave town. And take Jordan with you. He's dead.'

He called to the liveryman.

'Is there a doctor in town?' he asked.

A man who had walked up to stand by Turner, replied.

'I'm Doctor Parry,' he said.

'Would you take a look at Jordan and his friend?' asked Brad.

'Sure,' said the doctor.

He stepped on to the boardwalk and bent over Jordan. 'You were right about this one,' he said. 'He's dead.'

He moved over to Purdy and took a look at his injured arm. He turned to Brad.

'There's no bullet in the arm,' he said, 'but the flesh is badly torn. The arm ain't going to be much use for a while. I'll take him along to my place to treat the wound. Shouldn't take long.'

'He'll be fit to ride when you're finished with him?' asked Brad.

'Sure,' said Parry.

Brad spoke to Purdy and Dawson.

'I'm keeping your guns,' he said, 'and as soon as the arm's fixed, you'll do like I said, and both leave town. You'll take Jordan's body with you. It's up to you what you do with it.'

Both men, seething inwardly, stared at Brad.

'This ain't over yet,' said Purdy.

'If you've got any ideas about revenge, forget them,' said Brad. 'You won't get off so lightly next time.'

He accompanied the two men and the doctor to Parry's house. When Purdy's wound had been treated he made sure that the two men paid out any money due to the townspeople, before they rode out of town to the south, leading the horse carrying the body of Jordan. Then Brad returned to Turner and his wife, who were standing outside the livery stable.

'We both want to thank you,' said Martha Turner. 'We reckon that if you hadn't happened along it's likely Cal and me would've been in real trouble.'

'That's right,' said Turner, 'but we've been thinking that maybe, by helping us out like that, you've stirred up some serious trouble for yourself. You heard what Purdy said, and we know that Jordan and his brother Will were pretty close. It seems likely that Dawson and Purdy are going to let Will Jordan know what's happened to his brother. When that happens, it's likely that Jordan'll be out to get you.'

'You're probably right,' said Brad, 'and that could be useful because it so happens I'm looking for him.'

The Turners looked surprised.

'I'm going to tell you my reason for saying that,' said Brad, 'because I might need your help. But I'd like you to keep it to yourselves for the time being.'

'Sure,' said Turner, 'if that's the way you want it.'

'It's a long story,' said Brad, 'but

here's the gist of it. My name's Brad McLaine, by the way.'

He went on to tell them that he and his younger brother Cliff had recently been deputy sheriffs in West Kansas. Five weeks ago he and Cliff, after completing a mission, had been riding back to headquarters when they came across a westbound stagecoach which had been held up and robbed by four masked men about an hour earlier.

One of the three male passengers had said that the robbers had shot the driver while stopping the coach, and had ridden off to the south when the robbery was completed. The driver had died just before the arrival of the two deputies, but before doing so he told the passengers that he had recognized the leader of the robbers when his mask slipped down for a moment. He was Will Jordan, whose picture he had seen on Wanted posters. And the driver had said that another member of the gang, noticeably short, must have been a man called Harker.

One of the passengers, with driving experience, had offered to drive the stage to the next station, which was a home station, with the driver and the other passengers on board. When the stage arrived there the agent would be asked to send a message to the county sheriff, advising him of the situation.

This enabled Brad and Cliff to take off after the robbers, who would hardly be expecting that the law was so hard on their heels.

Following the outlaws' tracks to the south, the two deputies had arrived at a point where the gang had split up, two of them staying on the trail which led to the small town of Tasco, the other two heading in a direction which would bypass the town. Brad had followed the tracks leading into town, while Cliff had followed the others.

They arranged to meet early the following morning at a tall isolated rock outcrop which they knew existed a little way off the trail that headed south from Tasco.

Darkness was falling as Brad rode into town. At the store he heard about two strangers, fitting the descriptions of Jordan and Harker, who had called in for some provisions, and had left over an hour since. The storekeeper had not seen the direction in which they were heading when they left town.

Brad told the Turners that he had decided to stay in town overnight, and leave at dawn for his rendezvous with Cliff at the outcrop. But when he reached it there was no sign of his brother. He waited there for two hours before deciding that something must be amiss. He rode back to the trail, then followed it southwards, looking for tracks.

Half an hour later, on a patch of soft ground, he saw the recent prints left by five horses moving south. It looked as though the outlaws had joined up again, and were being followed by Cliff.

Brad had followed the trail for a further mile, to a point where it skirted a rock-strewn area on which he spotted the remains of a camp-fire. He rode up to them. It was clear that several men, possibly the Jordan gang, had camped there very recently.

Circling the area round the ashes of the fire, he found the place where the horses had been picketed. Close by was a patch of brush which looked as though it had been disturbed recently.

Brad paused before continuing his story, which the Turners had listened to in silence. Then he went on to tell them how curiosity had prompted him to push his way into the brush for a few feet, before stopping dead as he saw, close to his feet, the upturned face of his brother. The eyes were closed and the head was motionless. Forcing his way further into the brush, Brad picked up his brother, and retreated with the body, which was naked from the waist up. He laid it on the ground outside the brush.

As Brad had knelt down by his brother, he could see more clearly the battered face, the multiple bruises on the chest and sides, and the bullet wound on the chest. Half-turning the body over, Brad caught his breath and winced as he saw the mass of weals crisscrossing his brother's back. Then, as he held Cliff in his arms, he had heard the faintest of groans, and had discovered that his brother was still breathing.

'Somehow,' Brad told the Turners, who were listening intently to his story, 'the outlaws must have realized they were being followed, and they managed to capture Cliff. They beat him up and tortured him before shooting him and leaving him for dead.

'He was barely alive when I found him. He came to just for a few minutes, and told me that the men who had captured him were Jordan and his men Harker, Forrest and Devon. He said they all took turns at beating him before Jordan finally put a bullet in him. Then he passed out before he could tell me any more.

'I took him back to Tasco, and the

doctor there took him in and did everything he could for him. But he died the next day, without speaking again, just before the sheriff's posse arrived. And the outlaws were over the county line long before the posse could get anywhere near them.

'I buried Cliff and quit my job as deputy sheriff to go after the gang and hand them over to the law. Since then I've been looking for them. The reason I'm here is because I heard a rumour that they'd been seen in New Mexico Territory recently.'

'We're mighty sorry about your brother,' said Turner. 'What d'you aim to do now?'

'I'm going to follow Purdy and Dawson,' said Brad. 'I reckon that if Will Jordan's somewhere in the territory, there's a chance they'll be aiming to tell him about his brother's death. Maybe they'll lead me to him.

'But there's something you could do for me, just in case Jordan sends somebody to nose around here to find out something about the man who killed his brother, including his name. Would you please pass the word around town that my name's Rafferty, and that when I left town I was heading for South Texas?'

'Be glad to,' said Turner, 'and we wish you luck. That's a dangerous job you're taking on.'

2

Brad took his leave of the Turners and left town shortly after. It was not long before he came within sight of Dawson and Purdy, whose rate of progress was limited by the presence of the horse carrying Jordan's body.

Doing his best to ensure that the men ahead did not realize they were being followed, Brad continued his pursuit until just before nightfall, when he stopped as he saw them make camp by the side of the trail.

When darkness had fallen Brad saw the glow of a camp-fire ahead. He rode to within a few hundred yards of it, then dismounted and tethered his horse. He continued cautiously on foot, until he had reached a point from which he could watch Dawson and Purdy from cover.

The fire was burning brightly. As he

watched he saw the two men place the body of Jordan in a shallow depression in the ground close to the fire. Then, with Purdy working one-handed because of his wounded arm, the two men proceeded to cover the body with pieces of rock which were strewn around the area.

When they had finished they sat by the fire and took some food and drink. Brad was unable to get close enough to listen to their conversation. When they eventually lay down near the fire he returned to his horse and found a place where he could safely spend the night.

He woke well before dawn and continued to follow Purdy and Dawson when, shortly after daybreak, they rode on. They were still heading south-west. During the day they crossed the border into the Texas Panhandle. Once again, when they camped for the night, Brad was unable to get close enough to listen to their conversation.

The following morning the two riders veered slightly towards the south, and Brad judged that they were passing to the west of Amarillo. Once again they camped for the night, and on the following morning they followed a well-defined trail to the south for four miles before branching off to the right. Thirty minutes later they disappeared from Brad's view into what looked like a small isolated hollow.

Brad stayed where he was, and fifteen minutes later he saw Dawson and Purdy leave the hollow and head in his direction. Perhaps, he thought, they had expected to find somebody in the hollow, and had been disappointed. Hastily, he led his horse further into the gully in which he was hiding and watched the two riders as they rode back towards the trail they had recently left.

He waited till they had disappeared from view, then rode quickly to a point near the rim of the hollow. He dismounted, crawled forward and looked down into the hollow. He could see no men or horses.

He rode down into the hollow, and

soon discovered signs that several men had quite recently been staying there. He left the hollow and rode after Dawson and Purdy. He caught sight of them just as they were rejoining the trail. They rode along it in a southerly direction. Brad started to follow them again, and two hours later he spotted ahead, in the distance, the small town of Wesley. It lay on flat ground, with a low ridge to the east and a similar one to the west.

Brad watched the two riders ahead as they entered the town and disappeared from view. Then he headed for a gap in the low ridge to the west, and rode into it. Near the far end of the gap he rode into a winding gully stretching down from the top of the ridge.

He tethered his horse out of sight of anyone riding through the gap, then climbed to the top of the ridge, from which, through his field glasses, he had a good view of the town below. He settled down to watch for any sign of Dawson and Purdy leaving town.

At the same time, in Wesley, Ann Webster, wife of the telegraph operator, and her close friend Rachel Brand, wife of the liveryman, were mounting their horses outside the stable, preparatory to taking a recreational ride in the surrounding area. Both were attractive women in their early thirties, and both were accomplished horsewomen. This weekly ride in each other's company had become an enjoyable event in their lives.

They left town and headed for the gap in the ridge which Brad had ridden into earlier. They chatted as they rode along.

Brad saw them coming and kept his glasses trained on them. Turning, he watched them ride through the gap and on to the stretch of flat ground beyond. As they did so he suddenly stiffened. He had caught sight of two men standing on the ground ahead of the women riders. The two men were examining a foreleg on one of their horses.

The two women riders hesitated as they saw the two strangers in front of them. Then one of the men saw them. He called out and waved.

'Looks like they're in trouble,' said Rachel. 'Let's see what's wrong.'

As they reached the two men and looked at the horses they got the impression that the animals had been ridden almost to the limit of their endurance. And, looking at the two strangers, they sensed an air of desperation about them. Both were unkempt, with several days' stubble on their faces.

Before the women could react Rennie, the taller of the two, took hold of the bridle of Rachel's horse. At the same time his companion, Martin, grabbed hold of the bridle of Ann's mount. Then they roughly grabbed hold of the two women and pulled them out of their saddles. They both fell to the ground, and a moment later rose to their feet, to find that Rennie was holding a gun on them.

It was at that moment that Brad started moving down the gully.

'This is a fine pair of horses you've got here,' said Martin, a short, stocky man, 'and you couldn't have turned up at a better time. Both our mounts are plumb tuckered out, on account of that posse not far behind us. These two horses of yours'll suit us fine. We'll tie you up so's you can't raise the alarm. Then we'll be on our way. Likely somebody'll be out looking for you before nightfall.'

'You'll do no such thing!' said Ann, a spirited lady. 'Those are our favourite horses.'

'Too bad,' said Martin, advancing on Ann with a coil of rope in his hand. Incensed, Ann quickly leaned forward as he reached her and lifted his six-gun from its holster. But before she could turn it on him he struck her forcibly on the side of her jaw with his fist. Momentarily stunned, she dropped the gun, staggered sideways a few steps, and collapsed on the ground. Rachel ran up to kneel beside her friend.

Rennie and Martin, their backs to the ridge, looked down at them. Rennie was still holding his gun in his hand. Just as Martin was about to bend down and pick up his gun, they started as they heard a voice coming from behind them.

'There's a gun on your backs,' shouted Brad. 'I want to see your hands up in the air, pronto.'

Rennie ducked and twisted round, intending to fire at the man behind him, but Brad sent a bullet into his opponent's gun hand before he had lined up his revolver on Brad. His gun fell to the ground. As the two women flattened instinctively on the ground Martin bent down to pick up his own gun, but as his hand stretched out for it Brad's second bullet kicked it out of his reach. He straightened up and turned to face Brad, his hands raised.

'You two ladies all right?' asked Brad, as they rose to their feet.

'I'm all right,' Rachel replied.

'I had a fist in my face,' replied Ann, 'and I guess it ain't improved my looks any. Otherwise, I'm OK. We were lucky you happened along. There's a posse on the heels of these two, and they were figuring to steal our horses. What do we do with them now? We live in Wesley, on the other side of the ridge.'

'These two men look dangerous to me,' said Brad, 'so let's tie them up good.'

Brad ordered the two men to lie on the ground. Then, with the women's help, and using the rope the men had been carrying with them, he bound Rennie's arms firmly to his sides and tied his legs closely together. Then he secured Martin in the same way. When this was completed, Brad led the two women out of earshot of the captives.

He told them his name, then gave them an account of his brother's death and his encounter, in Rogan, with Dawson and Purdy who, little more than an hour ago, had ridden into Wesley. He explained his plan to discover the whereabouts of Will Jordan by following Dawson and Purdy.

'They left their horses at the stable,' said Rachel. 'They told my husband that likely they'd be staying in town for a few days.'

'You'll understand why I can't ride into town just now,' said Brad. 'If Dawson and Purdy see me, my plan's likely to fail. If we sling these two prisoners over the backs of their horses and tie them on, will you lead them into town? I reckon the horses ain't too tired to get them there. And from what you say, a posse should be along soon to pick them up.'

'We'll do that,' said Rachel. 'Our husbands and some of their friends in town'll make sure they're still here when the posse turns up.'

'Tell your husbands I'm still hanging around here,' said Brad, 'but I'd be obliged if you'd tell everybody else that I've ridden on.'

'We'll do that as well,' said Rachel.

'I've just had a thought,' said Ann.

'My husband Luke is the telegraph operator in Wesley. Maybe those two men you've been following have sent off some telegraph messages that you'd like to know about. If they have, maybe Luke'll let you know what was in them. I know he ain't supposed to, but after what you did for us, maybe I can persuade him.'

'I'm mighty obliged,' said Brad. 'I'll sneak into town after dark to see if you've got any news for me.'

'All right,' said Ann. 'Our place is next to the livery stable. You'll see the sign. Knock on the door at the back, any time between eight and eleven this evening.'

The prisoners cursed as Brad, with the help of the two women, hoisted them across the backs of their horses and tied them in position. Then Ann and Rachel, leading the two horses carrying the prisoners, rode back through the gap in the ridge and on into town. Brad returned to the top of the ridge.

The arrival in Wesley of the two women and their prisoners caused quite a stir. The liveryman and telegraph operator, who happened at the time to be engaged in conversation outside the stable door, stared in astonishment as they saw the procession approaching them. As they ran to meet it, it came to a halt on the street.

They bent down to look at the faces of the two prisoners, then walked over to their wives, who had dismounted. A small crowd collected around them, including Dawson and Purdy, who had just left the saloon. The women explained the situation, without divulging Brad's name or the fact that he was still in the vicinity.

Webster looked at the angry bruise on his wife's face. 'You all right, Ann?' he asked.

She nodded. 'It could have been a lot worse,' she said, 'if that stranger hadn't taken a hand. He sure gave those two a lesson in how to handle a six-gun.'

'We've got to put a guard on these

two till that posse gets here,' said Brand. 'Let's put them in an empty stall in the stable. We'll get the doc to tend to that wounded hand, and we'll round up a few men to take turns with ourselves at standing guard.'

'Right,' said Webster, and he and the liveryman led the prisoners' horses into the stable, pulled the two men off their horses, and dragged them into an empty stall. Outside, darkness was just beginning to fall.

A little later, in the house behind the stable, Ann and Rachel told their husbands the full story of what had happened on the far side of the ridge, and they explained Brad's reason for wanting to stay outside town.

'I think that maybe I can help him,' said Webster. 'Those two men did send a telegraph message just over an hour ago. I'll tell McLaine what was in it when he turns up.'

Later in the evening Brad rode into town, keeping in the shadows, and knocked on the rear door of the telegraph operator's house. Ann Webster let him in and introduced him to her husband. They all sat down in the living-room.

'I want to thank you,' said Webster, 'for what you done out there today. That sure is a mean-looking pair that you got the better of. Ann's told me what you're doing here, and I think there's something I can do to help you.

'The two men who rode into town just before Ann and Rachel left sent a telegraph message after they'd stabled their horses. I ain't supposed to do this, but I'm going to show you a copy of the message they sent. You can keep it if you want.' He handed the copy to Brad, who thanked him, then studied it carefully.

The message was addressed to J. HART, SALOON, LESTER, INDIAN TERRITORY. The message read: BRETT SHOT DEAD BY UNKNOWN MAN IN ROGAN NEW MEXICO. PURDY INJURED. WAITING INSTRUCTIONS FROM WJ. REPLY TO ME AT HOTEL IN WESLEY TEXAS

PANHANDLE. DAWSON.

'This is mighty interesting,' said Brad. 'WJ is obviously Will Jordan. And Lester's a small town west of here, well into Indian Territory, and about fifty miles south of the Kansas border. It looks like Will Jordan might be in hiding somewhere near there, and this J. Hart must know exactly where he is. I'd sure appreciate it if you'd let me see the reply to this telegraph message when it gets here.'

'I'll be glad to,' said Webster, 'but you may have to wait a few days.'

'All right,' said Brad, 'I'll go back to the ridge and ride into town each evening to see if a reply's turned up.'

'No need for that,' said Ann. 'We've got a spare room here. You can stay out of sight in the house till the message arrives. You can eat here with us. And I'm sure Tom Brand'll be glad to stable your horse for the time being.'

'I accept your offer,' said Brad, 'and I'm mighty obliged to you.'

When the posse turned up the

following morning Brand took them into the stable to see the prisoners. The leader of the posse, Ranger Dantry, eyed them with grim satisfaction.

'These are the two men we're after,' he said. 'They were rustling cattle on a ranch north of Amarillo, and they killed the rancher when he caught them in the act.'

He asked Brand how the pair had come to be caught. The liveryman told him what had happened on the other side of the ridge, and said that the stranger who had taken them prisoner had ridden on without giving his name.

'A pity,' said Dantry, 'I'd sure have liked to thank him for catching these two men for us.'

Later in the day the rangers departed with the two prisoners.

The reply to the telegraph message came three days later, around noon, and shortly after its arrival Webster handed a copy of it to Brad. It read: WJ SENDING WILSON TO DEAL WITH

MATTER. WAIT FOR HIM AT WESLEY. HART.

'D'you know this man Wilson?' asked Webster.

'I sure do,' Brad replied. 'He's a gun-fighter whose gun is for hire. He's very tall, and slim. Always dresses in black and carries two ivory-handled revolvers. He'll take on any dirty job if the pay is right. Most of the time he works alone.

'He used to be a bounty hunter before he turned to crime, and he had a reputation for always getting his man. I did hear a while back that he and Will Jordan were friendly, and that now and then he joined up with the gang for one of their operations.

'What're you planning to do now?' asked Webster.

'I'm going to Lester,' Brad replied. 'It's a long ride, but I'm hoping Jordan'll still be around when I get there. If he ain't, maybe I can get on his trail. I'll leave right now, but I'll have to make sure Dawson and Purdy don't see me.'

'That's easy,' said Webster. 'Ten minutes ago I saw them both go into the saloon on the other side of the street. They've been spending a lot of time in there. Get your horse and ride out of town behind the buildings lining the street. That way, there's no danger of them seeing you.'

Fifteen minutes later Brad left town.

3

Three days later when Brad rode into Lester, in Indian Territory, he left his horse at the livery stable, then took a room at the hotel. It was late afternoon. He asked Weston, the hotel owner, whether there was a J. Hart living in town.

'Sure,' said Weston. 'He owns the saloon on the other side of the street. He's probably in there now.'

Half an hour later Brad walked over to the saloon and passed through the swing-doors. Inside were a couple of customers seated at a table, and the barkeep, standing behind the bar. Brad walked up to him.

'I'm looking for Mr Hart,' he said.

'Wait here,' said the barkeep, and went into a room behind the bar. He came out shortly after, followed by a short man, bearded and neatly dressed, who walked round the end of the bar, then up to Brad.

'I'm Hart,' he said. 'What can I do for you?'

'Can we talk in private?' asked Brad.

Hart led the way to a table at the end of the room. They both sat down.

'Is Will Jordan around?' asked Brad. 'I need to see him.'

Hart's eyebrows lifted, and he looked hard at Brad.

'That name don't mean nothing to me,' he said. 'What made you think I knew this Jordan?'

'Only the fact,' said Brad, 'that you got a telegraph message from Dawson that you passed on to Will Jordan, and that you sent a reply back to Dawson. I have copies of these two messages with me.'

Startled, Hart eyed Brad suspiciously. 'Who are you?' he asked.

'My name don't matter,' Brad replied. 'All you need to know is that I want to find Jordan, and you're the man who's going to tell me where he is.'

Hart reached inside his jacket for the derringer stowed away in a shoulder-holster.

'I wouldn't,' said Brad. 'There's a Colt. 45 aimed at your belly under the table.'

Hart froze, then slowly withdrew his hand from inside his jacket and placed both hands on the table.

'That's better,' said Brad. 'Now let me make it clear just what you're going to do. I know you have contact with Will Jordan and his gang, and you're going to tell me exactly where they are.'

Hart had the appearance of a worried man. 'Why d'you want to know?' he asked.

'I'm waiting,' said Brad.

'And if I don't tell you?' asked Hart.

'The copies of the two telegraph messages that I'm holding will go to the US marshal at Fort Smith, Arkansas, with a report from me. There ain't no doubt in my mind that he'll have you picked up and taken to Fort Smith for trial before Judge Parker, for aiding known criminals.

'If you tell me what I want to know, I'll say nothing to anybody about you being tied up with Jordan, and I'll tell nobody that you helped me to find him. But if I find out that you've lied to me, you can be sure you'll end up in prison.'

Desperately, Hart considered the situation in which he found himself. Then he shrugged his shoulders.

'All right,' he said, 'but let me tell you first that I knew Jordan in Arkansas twelve years ago, before he got a gang together. He and I did a couple of robberies together. In the second one Jordan shot a bank-teller, though we'd agreed there was to be no shooting. We got away, and the teller recovered all right, but I decided to go straight, and me and Jordan parted company. After that I had a fair amount of luck at gambling, and I managed to put enough together to set up this saloon here.

'When Jordan and his men first

started using a hide-out near here about six months ago, Jordan found out that I'd set up in business here, and he got word to me to ride out to the hide-out to see him. When I did that he said he wanted me to help out by sending and receiving telegraph messages for him, and getting provisions out to the hide-out. If I didn't do what he wanted, he said, he'd make sure that the law got to know that I was involved in those two robberies in Arkansas. That's why I've been helping them. The fact is, the gang was hiding out in a ravine eight miles to the west. But they left it two days ago.'

'Where were they going?' asked Brad, 'and remember what I said about you lying to me.'

'They were heading for the Chisholm Cattle Trail east of here,' said Hart. 'They'd joined up with the Laker gang, that's Laker, Murray and Flint, with the idea of stealing a trail herd of two thousand longhorns belonging to the Box D Ranch in South Texas. The trail herd is heading for Caldwell, Kansas.

'I knew about the herd because the information was given in a telegraph message to Jordan from a man in Fort Worth called Wellman. The message also said that there were seven men with the trail herd, and that it would be about half-way through Indian Territory by today, if nothing held it up.

'Jordan told me that they were going to locate the herd, then shadow it until it was about eighteen miles south of the Kansas border. Then the two gangs would take it over and deliver it to a buyer who would take it without asking any questions. Who that buyer is, I don't know.'

'Is Wilson on his way to Wesley in the Panhandle yet?' asked Brad.

'He came to see Jordan at the ravine,' said Hart, 'and he left the same time as Jordan and the others. As far as I know he was going straight to Wesley. You've got to believe that everything I've just told you is the truth. I'm tired of being forced by Jordan to help him. I'd like to see the law get its hands on him and his gang.'

Brad was inclined to believe the saloon owner. He left Hart and went to the hotel for a meal. The following morning he bought some provisions, then rode out of town, heading east in the direction of the Chisholm Trail.

The trail was named after a Scottish-Cherokee trader called Jesse Chisholm, who had opened up a wagon road between his trading post on the Canadian River in Indian Territory, and Kansas. The Chisholm Trail had later become part of the route followed by millions of longhorns driven from cattle ranches in South Texas to railheads in Kansas, and other destinations beyond, during the post-Civil War era.

Brad planned to ride to a point on the Chisholm Trail around forty miles south of the Kansas border, where he would await the arrival of the Box D trail herd. When it arrived, he would warn the trail boss of the plan to steal the herd.

He knew that the herd would be moving northwards at a rate of ten to twelve miles a day, therefore he would probably have to wait a few days before it turned up at the point where he intended to wait.

Brad reached the Chisholm Trail during the morning of the following day. Trampled flat to a width of 200 yards or more, and bordered with the bones of cows which, for various reasons, had not survived the long journey, it was an unmistakable feature of the landscape. There were signs that a trail herd had passed along it recently.

Brad looked round for a vantage point from which he could watch out for the herd. Half a mile to the south, on the east side of the trail, a short, low, flat-topped ridge ran parallel to it. He rode up to the ridge, then along the foot of its eastern side until he found a narrow gully where he could conceal his horse. He rode up the gully, dismounted, and tethered his horse. Then he climbed to the top of the ridge and found a small hollow from which he had a good view of the cattle trail. There were no trail herds in sight at the time. Brad settled down to await the arrival of the Box D herd.

The following day a herd passed by, but it was only around 1000 head, with a five-man outfit — too small to be the Box D herd. Another small herd passed by the following day, then, two days after that, Brad saw, in the late afternoon, a herd of about 2000 head approaching. This, he thought, could be the trail herd he was waiting for.

He watched as the herd gradually came to a halt at the bed-ground selected by the trail boss for the approaching night. He saw the trail hands manoeuvre the herd into a circular formation, while the cook opened the chuckbox on his wagon, and lit the fire needed for preparing supper. Brad counted seven men with the herd.

He waited for an hour, then went down for his horse and rode to the camp. He called out as he approached the camp-fire. Four men were seated near it; the cook was busy near the chuck wagon. The remaining two men were with the herd, a little way off the trail, bedding the cattle down.

The men seated near the fire looked surprised to see Brad. One of them, a tall, rangy, sandy-haired man, rose to his feet. He eyed Brad suspiciously.

'Is this the Box D trail herd?' Brad asked.

'It is,' the tall man replied. 'I'm Hix, the trail boss. I'm curious to know what you're doing here.'

'My name's McLaine,' said Brad. 'Have you heard of the Jordan and Laker gangs of outlaws?'

'I've heard of the Jordan gang, but not the other one,' replied Hix.

He was about to continue when one of the trail hands cut in. His name was Morse.

'I've heard of the Laker gang, Mr Hix,' he said. 'A couple of years back I was in Denver, Colorado, when they

46

robbed a stagecoach between Denver and Pueblo, and killed the driver.'

'I'm wondering,' said Hix, 'just what those two outlaw gangs could have to do with us.'

'Well,' said Brad, 'the two gangs have joined forces, and they plan to steal this herd you're driving. There'll be seven of them all told. They're following behind you now, and they plan to take the herd when you're about eighteen miles south of the Kansas border. The reason I'm here is to warn you about what they're planning to do. And I'm hoping I can help to capture those outlaws and hand them over to the law.'

'I ain't seen no sign of anybody following us,' said Hix. 'How do we know you're telling the truth?'

'By listening to what I'm going to say,' Brad replied, and went on to tell his audience about the murder of his brother, his pursuit of the Jordan gang, and his encounter with a man in Lester whose name he had promised not to divulge.

'This man told me,' said Brad, 'what the two gangs were planning to do. And he also told me about a telegraph message that Jordan received, not long ago, from a man called Wellman in Fort Worth. The message said that the Box D trail herd should be halfway across Indian Territory about six days ago. Does the name Wellman mean anything to you?'

'It sure does,' replied Hix, grimly. 'He was running the store in Fort Worth where we bought some supplies when we were passing by. I recollect him asking me when we'd reach the crossing at Red River Station, and how long it would take us to cross Indian Territory. At the time, I figured it was just idle curiosity, but it looks like I was wrong. Come to think of it, there was a shifty sort of look about him.'

He pondered for a moment, while the trail hands rose to their feet and the cook joined the group. Then he spoke to Brad.

'I believe what you just told us,' he

said. 'It ain't ever happened to me, but I've heard of trail herds being stolen before. You any idea how many men we're up against?'

'Four in the Jordan gang and three in the Laker gang,' Brad replied, 'and they're all used to handling guns. And not one of them would think twice about shooting an innocent man down if he got in the way.'

'I can see we've got a big problem,' said Hix, well aware that, in general, the cowboy's Colt revolver would stay in the bunkhouse or in his bedroll during a trail drive, and would not usually be carried by him while he was at work. It was also a fact that shoot-outs between cowboys themselves were exceedingly rare. Consequently, the trail hands' performance in the use of the weapon would be no match for that of the outlaws they were about to face.

He turned to Brad.

'You just told us you'd been a deputy sheriff in Kansas,' he said. 'You got any

49

ideas about how we should tackle this situation?'

'Counting myself and the two men with the herd,' said Brad, 'that makes eight of us to deal with the outlaws. I expect they ain't that far behind the herd, and I aim to ride out now to find their camp. Maybe I can get near enough to them to find out something about the way they plan to steal the herd. If I can find out just when they plan to move in on us, maybe we can surprise them.'

Brad went on to suggest a plan he had worked out for dealing with the outlaws, provided he got the information he was after.

'It sounds good to me,' said the trail boss.

'What weapons and ammunition d'you have with you?' asked Brad.

'Each man has his own six-gun,' Hix replied, 'and there are three Winchester rifles in the chuckwagon. As for ammunition, we have enough for a short gun-battle, no more than that.'

'I brought some with me, just in case,' said Brad, 'but maybe we can get by without too much gunplay. I'm leaving now, to see if I can locate the outlaws' camp. I'm hoping they'll have a camp-fire burning. I'll come back later, to let you know what's happened.'

Brad rode south, parallel to the cattle trail, and a little way from it. He kept to the higher ground and paused frequently to scan the area in every direction. A mile and a half from the Box D camp he paused again, and this time he saw a faint glimmer of light ahead, well away from the trail.

He headed in that direction and twenty minutes later he was sure that the light came from a campfire. He rode on for a further five minutes, then dismounted and tethered his horse. Cautiously, he approached the camp. It was a dark night, with an overcast sky.

As Brad drew closer to the fire he heard the sound of voices and could see that the camp was sited on a piece of flat ground at the centre of which the campfire was burning with a strong, bright flame.

He circled the camp at a safe distance, and located the picketed horses, seven in all. Saddles and bridles were lying on the ground nearby. Circling a little further round the fire, Brad could see a large boulder, about five feet high, from behind which he would get the closest possible view of the men around the camp-fire, without being spotted.

He lay flat on the ground and inched his way towards the boulder, then crouched against it and cautiously peered round the side.

Seven men were seated on the ground close to the fire, talking among themselves in desultory fashion. Brad studied them one by one. He stiffened as the face of the tall, heavily built man he was looking at was illuminated by a spurt of flame from the fire. He was sure, from pictures he had seen of the outlaw, and from descriptions he had been given, that he was looking at Will Jordan.

Brad was too far away from the outlaws to be able to make out what they were saying. Frustrated by this, he continued to watch them from cover.

Thirty minutes passed, then a short man, who had been sitting next to the man whom Brad was sure he had identified as Jordan, rose to his feet. Brad suspected that this man was Harker. The man walked off in the direction of the horses. Half-way there, he stopped, felt in his vest pocket, and turned. He called out to the group of men he had just left. His words were clearly audible to Brad.

'I've just found out I've run out of tobacco,' he called out. 'D'you reckon, Will, that maybe we'll find some around the Box D camp when we take the herd over?'

The big man whom Brad had already assumed to be Will Jordan, replied. His words were clearly audible to Brad.

'There's bound to be some in the

chuckwagon for the trail hands,' he said. 'Just hang on till after midnight tomorrow, and you'll be able to smoke all you want.'

The man grunted and walked on towards the horses. He disappeared from Brad's view, to reappear after a few minutes and rejoin the others. Brad crawled away from the boulder until he could safely rise to his feet. He went for his horse and rode back to the Box D camp.

He arrived there at half an hour before midnight. He tied his horse to the picket-line, then walked towards the fire. Hix and the others, who had been anxiously awaiting his return, rose to their feet as he walked up to them.

'Any luck?' asked Hix.

'I found the outlaws' camp,' Brad told them. 'It ain't far south of here. All seven of them are there. And I had a stroke of luck. I overheard Jordan say that they were going to take the herd over tomorrow night, after midnight. I'll ride on ahead with you in the morning, and we'll pick out a place to camp tomorrow night that'll suit our plans.'

The following morning Hix and Brad left the trail hands as they were putting the cattle on the trail, and rode northwards along the trail at a steady pace. They had covered nine miles when Brad saw, ahead of them, a little way off the trail to the east, a stretch of flat ground covered with several thick, closely spaced patches of brush. He pointed it out to Hix.

'Let's take a look,' he said. 'That could be a good place to camp tonight.'

They rode up and examined the area. There was space at the centre for the camp-fire, the chuckwagon, and the bedrolls of the trail hands. The nearby patches of brush were dense, and not more than three and a half feet tall.

'This looks just right,' said Hix. 'We'll set up camp here tonight.'

Less than a mile off the trail, to the east, some hilly ground was visible.

'Let's take a look at that,' said Brad. They rode up to it and quite soon came upon a box canyon which they rode into and examined.

'We ain't going to find anything better than this,' said Hix. 'Let's go back to the herd.'

When they reached the herd they stayed with it until it reached the proposed campsite. The hands drove the herd off the trail, and bunched the cows. They held them there until darkness had fallen. Then, with Hix guiding them, they drove the herd up to and into the canyon which Brad and the trail boss had examined earlier in the day. The plan was that the herd would spend the night there, with no danger of a stampede being caused by the impending encounter with the outlaws.

One hand was left at the canyon entrance to guard the herd, with orders to fire three rifle shots in the air if there was any sign of strangers approaching the canyon. Hix and the remaining hands returned to the camp.

The cook had a fire going, and the

chuckwagon was standing nearby. Supper was ready in half an hour; when it had been taken Brad and Hix discussed their plan of action with the cook and the trail hands. Then they set to work. They looked at all the patches of brush surrounding the fire, and cleared five spaces within the patches where a man could hide in ambush. Then they rolled out five bedrolls on the ground, one near the chuckwagon, the rest at various points around the fire.

They cut out sufficient brush to form five rolls, each about five feet long and secured with rope. On each bedroll they placed a roll of brush and covered it with a blanket. Only close scrutiny could reveal that each blanket was not covering a sleeping man.

An hour before midnight Brad, three trail hands and the cook carried their weapons into the brush and took up their positions there. They settled down to await the arrival of the outlaws.

Hix and one of his trail hands,

Morse, carrying their weapons and lariats, rode out of camp and headed for a large shallow basin which lay east of the trail, and fairly close by. The track leading into the basin passed between two tall rock outcrops. They rode a little way into the basin, picketed their horses, and walked back to stand by the outcrops, straining eyes and ears for the first signs of the arrival of Jordan and the others.

At forty minutes past midnight the seven outlaws approached the camp from the south. On catching sight of the camp fire, they rode on a little further, then dismounted and secured their horses. Jordan and Laker crept towards the fire until they could make out the five blanket-covered rolls of brush lying around it. Then they crept back to rejoin the others.

'There's five men sleeping near the fire,' said Jordan. 'The other two'll be guarding the herd somewhere nearby. Me and Harker'll 'tend to them.'

He paused as the faint sound of a

song drifted in from a point somewhere east of the trail.

'That'll be one of the hands with the herd,' he said. 'Give us twenty minutes to locate them, then the rest of you can rush the camp. Those men sleeping around the fire'll be sitting ducks.'

Laker nodded, and watched Jordan and Harker as they rode off into the darkness in the direction of the sound of the distant song.

Twenty minutes passed, then Laker gave the word. He and the others ran towards the fire. They split up as they came nearer, each outlaw targeting one of the blanketed forms lying on the ground. Watched by Brad and the others, they launched a murderous attack on what they believed to be five sleeping men. Each outlaw fired several pistol shots into the blanket lying on the ground in front of him.

Just as the firing stopped the bundle of brush rolled from under the blanket at Laker's feet. He opened his mouth to shout out a warning to the others, but before he could do so a hail of fire from the five men hiding in the brush cut them down. Brad's companions fired without compunction, knowing that except for Brad's intervention they would have been murdered in their sleep. When the shooting stopped all the outlaws, who had been caught completely unawares, lay wounded on the ground. Brad's superior shooting-skill had done most of the damage, and he shouted to the wounded men to stay still.

Warily, Brad and the others moved out of the brush patches, holding their revolvers, and walked up to the men on the ground. They took their six-guns, and quickly checked for concealed weapons. Then one of the hands threw more wood on the fire, while Hendry the cook, as the medical expert in the outfit, holstered his gun, lit an oil-lamp from the chuckwagon and checked the five men lying on the ground.

He found three of them, Forrest, Devon and Murray, dead. Flint had been hit twice in the chest, and looked to be in a bad way. Laker, the last one the cook looked at, lay motionless on the ground, his forehead covered with blood. To Hendry it looked as though he had been fatally shot through the head.

But Laker was far from dead. He had recovered from the bullet-graze which had sent him down, and was closely watching Hendry through slitted eyes. The cook, kneeling beside Laker, twisted round as one of the hands called to him. Laker quickly reached out with his right hand and lifted Hendry's six-gun from its holster, then started to bring it round to bear on the cook.

Brad, standing not far from Hendry, and still holding his gun in his hand, shouted a warning to the cook. Laker reacted by turning his gun on Brad. Both men fired at the same time. Laker received a fatal wound in his chest, while Brad took a bullet wound in his left leg, which sent him to his knees.

The cook picked up his gun which had fallen from Laker's hand, and made sure that the outlaw was dead. Then he turned his attention to Brad, who had risen, shakily, to his feet.

With the help of the lamp the cook closely inspected the leg-wound.

'Your luck's in,' he said. 'There's a bullet in there, but it ain't that deep. I reckon it'll come out pretty easy. I'll tend to it as soon as I can. I reckon that if it hadn't been for you, I'd have got that bullet myself. I made a big mistake, thinking he was dead.'

'I don't see Jordan or Harker here,' said Brad. 'They must have ridden on to look for the herd. Let's hope Hix and Morse bring them in soon.'

'You'd best lie down till I tend to that leg,' said the cook. 'If you don't, you'll likely fall down.'

Hendry took another look at Flint, to find that he had died during the last few minutes. He turned to Brad.

'That leg won't take no harm for a little while,' he said. 'We'd better wait for the trail boss and Morse before I start work on it.'

* * *

Hix and Morse, each standing behind one of the two rock outcrops at the entrance to the basin, awaited the appearance of the outlaws. To lure them in the right direction, Morse was giving a rendition, repeated at intervals, of his favourite cattle-calming song, 'Dinah had a wooden leg'. This ditty, he claimed, could be guaranteed to relax the bovine nervous system.

It was a clear night, with a waning moon. Morse came to the end of his song, during which he had kept the volume well down to suggest that the herd was located well beyond the outcrops. As the song ended, Hix saw the outlines of two riders approaching from the direction of the camp.

'They're coming,' he called out softly to Morse: 'Two riders.'

'I see them,' said Morse.

As Jordan and Harker rode slowly, side by side, between the outcrops and into the basin, Hix and Morse slipped out behind them. Each of them was carrying a lariat. Each of them was highly proficient in the roping of cattle. The targets of Hix and Morse were Jordan and Harker respectively.

The loops fell simultaneously over the heads, and down over the shoulders, of the two outlaws. Morse braced himself, jerked the loop tight around Harker's arms and chest, and pulled the outlaw out of the saddle. Keeping the loop tight, he ran up to the outlaw, held a gun against his head, and relieved him of his revolver, which he threw aside.

Hix also tightened his loop and was well on his way to unseating Jordan when he stumbled over a stone half-embedded in the ground, and lost his balance. The rope slackened, and Jordan was able to lift the loop over his head and urge his mount forward into the darkness. Before Hix had gathered himself together the outlaw was out of sight.

As he rode through the basin, Jordan found no sign of the herd and he began to suspect that the plan to steal the cattle had been discovered, and that a trap had been set for him and the others. He stopped at the far side of the basin, and looked behind him. He could see or hear no signs that he was being pursued. Then he heard a burst of gunfire from the direction of the camp. It ceased, and there was silence for a while. Then he heard a single shot, after which there was silence again.

Watching out for any signs of pursuit he waited a further ten minutes for the signal, pre-arranged with the outlaws at the camp, of four rifle shots, equally spaced. This signal would indicate that Laker and the others had taken care of the five Box D men at the camp. When no signal was received Jordan knew that the attempt to steal the Box D herd had failed. He figured he had better make himself scarce. He climbed out of the basin and headed west.

Hix and Morse heard the burst of gunfire as they were tying Harker's hands together. The single shot came as they and their prisoner were mounting their horses. They rode back towards the camp. They approached it with caution, but soon established that the outlaws had been defeated.

They joined the others by the camp-fire, where the cook, with the aid of an oil-lamp, was taking a closer look at Brad's wound. They told them how one of the two outlaws who had been looking for the herd had escaped.

'That's Harker you've got with you,' said Brad, 'which means that Jordan's got away. My guess is that he ain't going to hang around here, but just in case, we'd better post guards on the camp.'

This was done, then the cook got his medicine-box from the chuckwagon and heated up some water. He sterilized his instruments in the fire, then probed for the bullet in Brad's leg and removed it. He showed it to his patient.

'I'm sure glad that's out,' said Brad.

The cook cleaned the wound and bandaged it up.

'There's a good chance that'll heal up all right,' he said, 'but only if you do no walking or riding for a spell. I'll clear a space in the chuckwagon where you can rest up. We should be in Caldwell day after tomorrow. You'll be able to see a doctor there.'

'Thanks,' said Brad. 'We can hand Harker over to the law there. After that, as soon as I can ride, I'll be on Jordan's trail again.'

'I ain't forgotten,' said Hix, 'that if it hadn't been for you we'd likely have lost the herd and maybe our lives as well. If there's any way we can help you, let me know.'

At daybreak they buried the dead outlaws. Two days later they reached Caldwell and Hix delivered the herd to the buyer. Harker was handed over to the county sheriff, who was told about the attempt to steal the herd.

Brad was taken to Doc Mitchell, who took a good look at the gunshot wound.

'That's coming along fine,' he said, 'but you're going to be laid up another week. I can put you up here if you like.'

Gratefully Brad accepted the offer, and four days later he was visited by Hix and the Box D trail hands, who were aiming to leave for the Box D in Texas the following morning.

'You decided where you're heading when you're fit to ride?' asked Hix.

'I've been thinking about that,' said Brad, 'and I'm aiming to ride back to Lester, where I found out about the plan to steal the trail herd. I need to pass on the news that Jordan's on the loose, and there's a chance I can get some information that'll help me to find him. As it is, I've no idea where he was heading when we lost him.'

'I sure hope you find him again,' said Hix, 'and if you ever happen to be anywhere near the Box D, you be sure to drop in and see us.'

'I'll do that,' said Brad.

4

Four days later Mitchell pronounced Brad fit to ride. Brad thanked the doctor and headed for Lester, which he reached the following day. He tied his horse to a hitching-rail outside the saloon and went inside.

Hart, standing behind the bar with the barkeep, started as he saw Brad come in. He motioned him to follow him into the room behind the bar. He closed the door behind them.

'News just got in about the raid on the Box D trail herd,' he said. 'Is it right that five of the outlaws are dead, and that one of them whose name we don't know, got away?'

'That's right,' said Brad, 'and the one who got away was Jordan. I've got two reasons for coming here. First, I wanted to warn you that Jordan's on the loose. He's probably gone to some place where he can hide out safely for a spell. Nobody but you'n me knows that you told me where to find Jordan. But he'll be wondering how it was that a trap came to be set for him and the others. Maybe he'll start figuring that either you or Wellman at Fort Worth had something to do with it.'

'You've got me worried,' said Hart, 'but like you say, he'll probably be lying low for a spell, and maybe you'll catch up with him before he decides to pay me a visit.'

'My second reason for coming here,' said Brad, 'is to find out if you can give me any idea of where I might find him. Where would he go when he's lost all his men? It goes without saying that it'll be in your own best interest if you can help me out on this.'

Hart thought hard for a few moments before answering.

'Jordan once told me,' he said, 'that he owned a cattle ranch, but he didn't say where it was located. Then, the last time I visited the hide-out, not long before they all left to follow the Box D herd, I overheard two of the outlaws talking. They didn't realize I was close by, and could hear what they said.

'They were talking about driving the stolen cattle to a Lazy Z Ranch in the Texas Panhandle, about sixty miles from Amarillo. I'm pretty sure from what I heard that the ranch is Jordan's, and I think it's a safe bet that he would head there when the operation failed.'

'That's a mighty interesting bit of information,' said Brad. 'You know which direction from Amarillo the ranch lies?'

'No, I don't,' Hart replied, 'only that it's about sixty miles away.'

'I'll ride to Amarillo, then,' said Brad, 'and find out just where the Lazy Z Ranch is located. Then I'll ride there and nose around to see whether Jordan's there. I'll let you know when I've finally located him and he's either dead or I've handed him over to the law.'

'I'll be obliged,' said Hart.

Four days later, around noon, Brad rode into Amarillo. He headed for the office of a big freighting company whose sign he could see along the street. He knew that the company operated throughout Texas. He dismounted outside the office and went in.

Horne, the agent, was seated at his desk. He looked up as Brad came in.

'Howdy,' he said. 'Something I can do for you?'

'I'm hoping so,' said Brad. 'I want to meet up with an old friend of mine who's working on a cattle ranch called the Lazy Z. I know that the ranch lies about sixty miles from here, but I don't know in what direction. I figured that maybe you would know.'

Horne sat back in his chair and closed his eyes as he searched his memory.

'The Lazy Z,' he repeated slowly. 'Let me think.'

Moments later, his eyes opened. 'I

think I know,' he said. 'About six months ago we freighted some timber to a ranch called the Lazy Z. Let me take a look at my records.'

He took a ledger out of one of the drawers in his desk and thumbed through the pages until he found what he was looking for.

'Here it is,' he said. 'The Lazy Z we delivered the timber to is near a small town called Barlow, fifty or sixty miles from here, to the south-east. The man running the place is called Paxton. I don't know of any other Lazy Z that distance from here.'

'I'm obliged to you,' said Brad. 'I'll take a meal, then head for the ranch. I'll camp out overnight.'

Just before noon the following day Brad was heading for Barlow which, he judged, was only a few miles ahead. He was riding over range well-stocked with cows carrying the Lazy Z brand.

A little way ahead of him he could see three horses, with two men standing close by them. The men appeared to be looking down at something on the ground. As Brad drew closer he could see that it was a young woman, raven-haired and attractive, and probably in her early twenties. Her dark eyes blazed with anger, and a grimace of pain showed on her face, as she looked up at the two men standing over her.

The men saw Brad approaching. They stood watching him as he reined in his mount nearby, dismounted, and walked up to them. The two men he stood facing were Lazy Z ranch hands, Tomkin and Rooney, both of them tough-looking characters, and each wearing a right-hand gun.

'Who're you?' asked Tomkin, abruptly, scowling at Brad.

'None of your business,' Brad replied.

He looked down at the young woman on the ground. She was holding her left ankle.

'Looks like you could do with some help, miss,' he said.

Tomkin cut in before the woman

could reply. His voice was harsh and threatening.

'And this is no business of yours,' he said. 'You're on Lazy Z range. You're trespassing. If you don't move on pronto, with no more argument, you're going to be sorry. The lady fell off her horse. We'll take care of her.'

Angrily, the woman spoke. 'I did fall off my horse,' she said, 'but only because Tomkin here thought it would be fun to lash my horse with his rope. As for these two bullies taking care of me, Tomkin is lying. He and Rooney are harassing me because the man who runs the Lazy Z can't get my father to sell our ranch to him.'

Brad spoke to the two men. 'You talk about me trespassing,' he said, 'but even though Lazy Z cows are grazing here, this range is still public land. You can't stop me or anybody else from riding over it.

'As for the lady, it's clear she don't want anything to do with the two of you, and I don't blame her. Any help she wants, she can get from me. You two ain't welcome here. I reckon you'd best be moving on.'

Tomkin's temper flared, and Rooney moved across to stand by his partner, facing Brad.

'You've sure got some gall,' said Tomkin. 'I reckon it's time to shut you up.'

He went for his gun. Mary Bellamy, sitting on the ground, watched wide-eyed as she saw Brad's Peacemaker appear miraculously in his right hand. Brad shot Tomkin in the right arm before the ranch hand was ready to fire.

Rooney, who had been confident that his partner was well capable of dealing with this meddlesome stranger, reached for his gun as Tomkin was hit, but the sight of Brad's cocked six-gun pointed at his head stopped his hand before he had completed his draw. He let the six-gun drop back into the holster.

Brad stepped forward and lifted Rooney's gun from its holster. Then he picked up the revolver which had fallen from Tomkin's hand when he was hit.

'I'll hang on to these,' he said. 'You two can leave now.'

The two men mounted, Tomkin with some difficulty. The wounded man, seething with rage, spoke to Brad.

'This ain't over yet,' he said.

'Get moving,' said Brad.

He and the woman watched as the two hands rode off in the direction of Barlow. Then Brad turned to Mary.

'I'm Brad McLaine,' he said, kneeling down beside her. 'Let me take a look at that ankle.'

'Mary Bellamy,' she said. 'I'm obliged for your help.'

Brad could see that the ankle was swollen; he felt it gently with both hands.

'My guess is,' he said, 'that it's not broken, but badly sprained, and you won't be walking on it for a while. I reckon a doctor should see it. Is there one anywhere near?'

'There's one at Barlow, five miles from here,' she replied. 'I'll go there and see Doc Marvin.'

Brad took a roll of bandage from his saddle-bag and wound it firmly around the injured ankle. Then he brought her horse, and helped her on to the saddle.

'You reckon you can ride with me to Barlow?' he asked.

'I'll be all right,' she replied. 'That bandage is helping. I'm sure glad you happened along. I can't tell you how much I enjoyed seeing those two cut down to size.'

Brad mounted and they set off for Barlow, choosing a pace which was not too painful for Mary.

As they rode along she told him that she and her parents ran the Circle B horse ranch on the other side of the northern boundary of the Lazy Z range. Mary said that over the last six months, Paxton, who ran the Lazy Z, had made several offers to her father for the ranch, but on each occasion it was made plain to him that her father had no intention of selling. When Paxton realized that the rancher was adamant in his refusal to sell, he adopted a threatening attitude and told Bellamy that he would either have to accept the offer or face the consequences.

Then, earlier that day, Tomkin and Rooney had intercepted her as she was riding towards Barlow. They had told her that she'd better get her father to change his mind and accept Paxton's offer. Then Tomkin had deliberately struck her horse on the flank and she had been thrown to the ground.

'I'm afraid of what they might do next,' she said, 'either to my parents or me.'

'I aim to hang around here for a while,' said Brad. 'Maybe I can help you.'

She looked across at him.

'I've seen what you can do,' she said, 'and I'm grateful. But as well as Tomkin and Rooney, Paxton has maybe ten other men on his payroll, all like the two men you outfought back there. And we only have three men helping out on the ranch, that's Leary and Perrin, and

Wes Bailey, our foreman, an old friend of the family. All three are pretty good with horses, but not so good at handling guns. So maybe you'd like to think again.'

'The offer still stands,' said Brad.

When they reached Barlow and rode towards the DOCTOR sign on a building along the street they saw Tomkin and Rooney leave the building and go into the saloon on the other side of the street.

Brad dismounted at the sign, helped Mary out of the saddle, and carried her inside. Doc Marvin, a short, cheerful, middle-aged man, looked closely at Brad before carefully examining Mary's ankle.

'That's a bad sprain, Mary,' he said, when he had finished. 'I'm pretty sure there's no fracture. What happened?'

Mary told him how she had been stopped and molested by Rooney and Tomkin, and how Brad had intervened.

'Tomkin just left,' said the doctor. 'Maybe you saw him. I patched up his arm. It's going to be quite a while before he can handle a gun properly again. It seems like Paxton and his men figure they can do just what they like around here.

'You'd best go back to the ranch in the buggy, Mary. It's not a good idea for you to ride a horse just now. I'll ride out in a couple of days to see how you're getting on. I can't drive you out myself, but I'll find somebody who can.'

'No need for that,' said Brad, 'I'll do it myself.'

'All right,' said Marvin, 'so long as I can have the buggy back tomorrow.'

After the doctor had finished bandaging the ankle Brad brought the buggy round to the door. He helped Mary inside. He tied their horses behind and they set out for the ranch. As they left town there was no sign of Tomkin and Rooney.

It was late in the afternoon when they arrived at the Circle B ranch house. Mary's parents, Josh and Grace

Bellamy, who had seen them approaching, came out of the house and walked up to the buggy as it came to a stop. Wes Bailey, the foreman, joined them. Surprised to see Mary inside the buggy, they looked curiously at her companion.

'I've hurt my ankle,' said Mary. 'Can't put any weight on it.'

Brad helped her into the arms of her father, who carried her into the house and deposited her on a couch in the living-room. The others followed.

Mary told her parents about the confrontation with the Lazy Z hands, followed by Brad's intervention. When she had finished, Bellamy, a slim, pleasant-looking man, turned to Brad.

'We're mighty beholden to you, Mr McLaine,' he said, 'for helping Mary like you did. I don't know how this is going to end. Paxton seems to be set on getting us to move out, whatever it takes.'

'Like I told Miss Bellamy,' said Brad. 'I aim to help you if I can.'

He went on to tell them of his brother's murder, his pursuit of the Jordan gang, and the possibility that Jordan might be on the Lazy Z.

'What I'm here to do,' he explained, 'is find Jordan and make him pay for what he's done. And maybe, at the same time, I can stop Paxton and his men from harassing you.

'I'd be obliged if all that I've just told you, you'd keep to yourselves for the time being. And while I'm here, I'm calling myself Jim Ford.'

'All right,' said Bellamy, 'but I must say it looks like a real dangerous job you've taken on. We'll help you any way we can.'

'What I've been thinking of doing,' said Brad, 'is trying to get a job on the Lazy Z. As far as I know, before I got here I'd never met up with anybody, including Jordan, who might be at the Lazy Z.'

The following morning, before driving the doctor's buggy back to Barlow, Brad had a few words with Mary. She told him that her ankle was a little better, and thanked him once again for his help.

'I'll stay in Barlow for the time being,' said Brad. 'Get word to me if you want any help out here.'

'I'm wondering if we'll ever see you again,' she said.

'You can count on it,' said Brad, 'and meantime, if I can, I'll let you know how things are going with me.'

After handing the buggy back to the doctor Brad took a room at the hotel, showing his name as J Ford in the register, At one o'clock in the afternoon he went into the hotel dining-room for a meal.

He had finished the meal and was just about to leave when the door opened and a man entered. He was well-dressed, middle-aged, and running a little to fat. He wore a neatly trimmed goatee beard. His face was bleak, his eyes hard. He stood for a moment, looking around the room, then headed for Brad's table. He stood, looking down at Brad.

'Mr Ford?' he asked.

Brad nodded.

'I'm Paxton,' said the man standing at the table. I run the Lazy Z Ranch north of here.'

He sat down.

'My men told me about that incident on the Lazy Z range yesterday,' he said. 'Tomkin's a fool, and Rooney's no better. They were harassing the Bellamy girl without my authority.'

'It wasn't so much the harassing of the girl that got me riled,' said Brad. 'It was the way Tomkin was ordering me around, just like a lawman. That's something I don't take kindly to. I don't like the way the law interferes with what we want to do nowadays. I hanker for the time when folks made their own laws.'

'From what my men told me,' said Paxton, 'it seems you're pretty handy with a gun. You certainly impressed them. I have a friend who can use a man like you. He has a job for you if you want it.'

'What kind of a job would that be?' asked Brad.

'It's a job,' Paxton replied, 'that needs plenty of nerve and a special talent with a six-gun. My friend'll let you know more about it if you feel like riding out to see him at the Lazy Z. As for the pay, the operation my friend's planning will bring in a lot of money, and you'll get a proper share. Think about it, and take a ride out to the ranch if you want to know more.'

'I'll do that,' said Brad.

He sat for a while after Paxton had left, wondering if the rancher's offer was just a ruse to get him out to the Lazy Z, so that they could take revenge for the shooting of Tomkin. But on reflection he felt sure that the offer was genuine. And there was a chance that Paxton's friend was Jordan. The opportunity of getting close to Jordan must not be missed.

He decided to ride out to the Lazy Z the following day, realizing that if his true identity was discovered he would be in serious trouble.

He went to the store and bought a

small pair of scissors, a needle and some thread. Outside the store he took out the pocket-knife which he carried with him and broke off one of the blades. He walked along the street to the blacksmith's shop and asked the blacksmith to put the sharpest possible edge on the blade.

The blacksmith took the blade to his treadle-operated sharpening-wheel. When he had finished he handed the blade to Brad.

'As near razor-sharp as I can make it,' he said, idly wondering for what purpose the blade was to be used.

'That's fine,' said Brad, as he felt the edge of the blade.

He paid the blacksmith, then returned to his room at the hotel where he busied himself with the items he had bought at the store.

5

Before Brad left Barlow for the Lazy Z, he handed a letter to the doctor and asked him to hand it to Bellamy the next time he called to see Mary. In the letter Brad told him of Paxton's offer of a job and said that he was riding out to the Lazy Z to follow it up.

He reached the ranch buildings late in the afternoon and rode up to the house. Paxton was standing outside the door, talking to one of the hands, who walked off as Brad rode up.

'Glad you decided to come,' said Paxton. 'The man who wants to talk with you is inside. Let's go and see him.'

Brad's face gave no hint of his expectation that his pursuit of Jordan might have ended at last. He followed Paxton into the living-room and, from descriptions he had been given, he immediately recognized the tall, stocky, bearded man with a scarred temple who was sitting in an armchair as Will Jordan, the man who had tortured and murdered his brother.

Controlling with difficulty the impulse to kill which welled up inside him, Brad accepted Paxton's invitation to sit down.

'This is Ford, Will,' said Paxton.

Jordan looked closely at Brad before speaking.

'From that talk you had with Paxton here,' he said, 'it seems that you ain't exactly a strong believer in the law.'

'The law and me,' said Brad, 'we ain't never seen eye to eye. I rode out here to find out more about the job that's on offer.'

'My name's Will Jordan,' said the outlaw. 'Maybe you've heard of me?'

Brad eyed Jordan closely before he replied.

'The leader of the Jordan gang, I seem to remember, was called Will. I'm guessing that's who you are.'

'You've guessed right,' said Jordan.

'The situation is, I had a bad stroke of luck not long ago, and I'm all that's left of the gang. I aim to build it up again, and it seems to me you're the kind of man I'm looking for. Two men from the Lazy Z, and another one who's arriving soon, will be joining me. So if you join me as well, we'll have a gang of five. Your share of the proceeds of a job I have in mind will make you a rich man. How does the idea of joining up with us strike you?'

'It sounds a very attractive proposition to me,' said Brad.

'Good,' said Jordan. 'The man I'm waiting for will be arriving here pretty soon. Then we'll be leaving the ranch. I have a job lined up not more than sixty miles from here that should make us all rich. Now I've got four good men with me, the job should be easy.

'Meanwhile, there's a small cabin near the bunkhouse you can use while you're here. And you can take supper in the cookshack at seven o'clock. We'll talk more about the job when we're all here. You might as well know that I own this ranch, and Paxton here runs it for me.'

Brad left the house, put his horse in the pasture, then went to the cabin near the bunkhouse. It was comfortably furnished, with a view of the house, cookshack and bunkhouse from the window. He lay down on the bed, trying to devise a plan which would enable him to capture Jordan and get him away from the Lazy Z without alerting Paxton and the hands.

Inside the bunkhouse were several men, one of whom was lying on a bunk with splints attached to his lower right leg. The man was Purdy who, with Dawson and Will Jordan's brother, Brett, had tangled with Brad in Rogan.

Purdy and Dawson had waited in Wesley for Wilson, the gunfighter sent by Will Jordan to hunt down the man who had killed his brother. When Wilson arrived they had given him a description of Brad and details of their encounter with him. Wilson had then left on his mission.

On the same day Dawson and Purdy parted company. Purdy headed for the Lazy Z, where he intended to ask Paxton for a job, while Dawson rode off to visit some relatives in Kansas.

On the day after he reached the Lazy Z, and was taken on by Paxton, Purdy was thrown from his horse when it lost its footing on a steep slope, and his right leg had been broken. Since then he had been confined to the bunk-house.

Jordan had been in to see Purdy, who gave him an account of the killing of his brother Brett. He also gave him a rough description of Brad, but could not remember any particular distinguishing features.

Later, when Jordan met Brad, the thought had never entered his head that the man he was talking to was the man who had killed his brother.

Purdy's leg was healing well, and he expected soon to be able to leave the bunkhouse. It was a little before nightfall when, tired of the inaction, he eased himself off the bunk, took hold of a pair of crutches, and moved over to the bunkhouse window.

As he stood there the cook came out of the cookshack to beat vigorously on the large triangle hanging just outside the door. Purdy's companions in the bunkhouse rose to their feet and left him alone. He knew that the cook would soon be bringing him his own supper.

He was just about to turn away from the window to go back to his bunk, when he saw the door of the nearby cabin open. A man came out and closed the door behind him.

As the man turned to face him, Purdy stiffened. He was sure that he was looking at the man Wilson was searching for. He watched as the man walked over to the cookshack and disappeared inside. Then he saw a ranch hand ride in from the range and approach the bunkhouse. When the hand came in, Purdy asked him to go to the house and tell Jordan that Purdy wanted to see him in the bunkhouse right away.

'It's urgent,' he said. 'I've got to talk to him right now. Tell him it won't wait.'

Five minutes later Jordan came into the bunkhouse.

'What's this urgent matter you want to talk to me about?' he asked.

'A few minutes ago,' said Purdy, 'I saw a man leave the cabin out there and go into the cookshack.'

'That would be Ford,' said Jordan. 'He's joining the gang.'

'The man I saw was the man who killed your brother,' said Purdy. 'I'm certain of it.'

Jordan was visibly shaken. 'You absolutely sure?' he asked.

'Absolutely,' replied Purdy. 'You say his name is Ford?'

'That's what he calls himself,' said Jordan, 'but maybe that ain't his real name. It seems like a big stroke of luck that you happened to be here to identify Ford. But I can't help thinking he ain't here by chance. He must know that I'm the brother of the man he killed. But just what is he doing here? Before we finish him off, I aim to find the answer to that question. You stay here out of sight. Paxton and me'll attend to Ford.'

When Brad walked into the cook-shack the cook, who was handing round some plates of food, motioned him to one of the three vacant seats at the large table, near that end of the table which was closer to the door. The men at the table glanced at him curiously, but made no effort to engage him in conversation.

Half-way through the meal the door opened and Jordan and Paxton walked in. The cook and the hands looked at them in surprise, aware that the duo invariably took their meals in the house.

The two men walked behind Brad, then suddenly turned and moved up behind him. Jordan jammed the muzzle of his six-gun into the back of Brad's neck. Brad, taken completely unawares, froze in his seat.

'Now, Ford,' said Jordan, 'pull out your six-gun, slow-like, with your thumb and finger, and lay it on the table.'

When Brad had done this Jordan ordered him to stand up. Paxton searched him for concealed weapons and removed the contents of his pockets.

'This man,' said Jordan to the hands, 'is the one who killed my brother Brett. Purdy saw him do it. What his reason is for being here, I don't know. But I aim to find out.'

Jordan and Paxton took Brad at gunpoint to the bunkhouse, where Purdy was lying on his bunk. He stared at Brad as they came in.

'Take a good look,' said Jordan. 'Can you definitely identify this man as the one who killed Brett?'

'I'd stake my life on it,' said Purdy.

Jordan and Paxton took Brad back to the cabin which he had recently left. Once inside, Jordan ordered Brad to sit on the floor with his back to the wall. Then he sat on the bed, facing his prisoner, while Paxton examined the contents of Brad's pockets. He then searched the room and Brad's saddle-bags. He was looking for anything which would help to establish Brad's identity and his reason for being there. But the search was fruitless.

Jordan spoke to Brad.

'You've saved me a lot of trouble, turning up here like this,' he said. 'It happens I have a man out looking for you. Now I can call him off. Like you heard me say already, I'm mighty curious about your reason for being here. You can tell us right now, and save us the trouble of beating the truth out of you. What's it to be?'

'Your brother was a bully and a fool,' said Brad, 'and what happened to him he brought on himself. As to why I'm here, it's just by chance I was riding across your range when I met up with Tomkin and Rooney. I was interested in the job on offer, but when I found out

I'd be riding with you I figured I'd be crazy to risk you finding out that I was the one who shot your brother. So I'd decided to slip away during the night, when nobody'd see me leave.'

'I don't believe you,' said Jordan. 'I'm certain you ain't here just by chance.'

He turned to Paxton.

'If we're to get this man talking, we need Pardoe in here,' he said.

'Pardoe's on the north range, looking at some sick cows,' said Paxton. 'He should be back early tomorrow.'

'For your information, Ford,' said Jordan, 'Pardoe's half-Indian. What he don't know about torture ain't worth knowing, and what's more, he really enjoys handing it out. Tomorrow we'll let him have a go at dragging the truth out of you.'

He turned to Paxton.

'We'll tie Ford up, and keep him in the cabin overnight,' he said. 'And we'll have a man on guard inside the cabin all night.'

'I'll go for Fletcher,' said Paxton. 'I'll

be back in a few minutes.'

He returned shortly after with Fletcher, one of the hands. Fletcher was armed, and was carrying a coil of rope. He tied Brad's upper and lower legs together, then, by circling the upper part of the prisoner's body with several turns of rope, he bound his arms firmly to his sides. He left Brad lying on his side, with his back to the wall, and anchored him in position by tying a rope round his neck and making it off around the leg of a heavy cupboard standing nearby, against the wall.

Paxton told Fletcher that he would arrange for relief guards to take over in four and eight hours' time, and he ordered him not to leave the cabin until his relief arrived. Then he and Jordan left.

It was growing dark outside, and Fletcher lit an oil-lamp. Then he sat on the bed with his back to a pillow resting against the headboard. From there he had a view of Brad, lying on the floor. He drew his six-gun and laid it on the bedside table near his right hand.

Two hours later, Fletcher, who apart from an occasional brief doze, had been watching the prisoner continuously, slid a little further down on to the bed. Watching him closely, Brad saw Fletcher's eyes close and his head drop back on the pillow. A gentle snore came from his direction. The ranch hand was asleep.

Brad, watching Fletcher closely, started out on the process of working his arms round towards the front of his body, so that his hands could meet. His arms were so tightly bound to his sides that progress was slow. But eventually his hands touched. Fletcher was still asleep.

Brad inserted the thumb and finger of his right hand inside his left shirt-sleeve and felt for the narrow pocket, sewn in place by him in Barlow, in which he had secreted the blade from his penknife. It took some time, but at last he was able to ease the blade out of the pocket and withdraw it from the sleeve, holding it firmly between finger and thumb.

He froze as the ranch hand's snore was momentarily interrupted, and Fletcher stirred in his sleep. Then, once again, the welcome sound of the snore reached Brad's ears.

Still keeping a close watch on the man on the bed, Brad cut through the rope around his arms. When both arms were free he cut through the rope between his neck and the cupboard and removed the noose from his neck. Finally he cut through the ropes binding his legs together. Fletcher was still slumbering peacefully.

Brad stood up, and flexed his arms and legs, stiff after their movement had been restricted for so long. Then, when his limbs seemed to be under control, he started moving silently towards the bed, his target being the six-gun on the bedside table. As he neared the foot of the bed his right leg suddenly gave way, and he lurched against the bed.

Fletcher was instantly awake. He

grabbed for his gun and cocked it. Brad was just in time to knock the gun from his hand as he fired. The gun fell on the bed.

The deflection of the shot was not enough to save Brad from injury. He was struck in the left side, above the hip. Ignoring the pain he grabbed for the six-gun, which had dropped near him, and struck Fletcher forcibly on the side of the head with the barrel of the gun. Fletcher fell back on the bed, unconscious.

Hurriedly, hoping that the sound of the single shot had not been heard outside the cabin, Brad bound Fletcher as securely as he could, with the rope that had been used on himself.

Then he gagged him. As he did so, his victim was showing signs of coming to. Brad took his Texas hat off a peg on the wall, and jammed it on. Then, taking his belongings and Fletcher's six-gun with him, he quietly closed the door behind him. There was no indication outside that the shot had been heard.

He ran to a covered walkway between the bunkhouse and the cookshack, where saddles and bridles were stowed. He felt for a bridle and picked one up. As he did so he saw a light come on in the bunkhouse. He abandoned his plan to take a saddle as well as a bridle with him. Trying to ignore the intense pain in his side, he ran to the pasture and entered it through the gate.

Moving slowly so as not to startle the animals, he put the bridle on the first horse he came to and led it to the gate. Looking back towards the bunkhouse, he saw light streaming through the open door momentarily, before it was closed; he guessed that his escape was about to be discovered. With the help of the pasture fence, he mounted the horse and headed away from the buildings.

Feeling his wounded side, he found that his shirt was soaked with blood. He decided to seek help at the Circle B, but first, in order to make his tracks more difficult to follow, he took a meandering path over a long stretch of hard ground which he had noticed on his way to the Lazy Z the previous day. Then he headed north for the Circle B.

He rode on for what seemed an eternity, swaying in the saddle, and growing weaker and weaker from loss of blood as time passed. Eventually, as his mind and body ceased to co-ordinate, he fell sideways from the saddle on to the ground. He made a feeble effort to rise, then slumped back to the ground and lay still.

*　*　*

At the Circle B Mary Bellamy rose early. She had spent a restless night after Brad's letter had arrived at the ranch house. She found herself feeling deeply concerned about the danger he must be facing at the Lazy Z.

It was just after sunrise. She moved over to the window, using a pair of makeshift crutches which her father had fashioned for her. As she stood looking out of the window towards the south, her attention was caught by the sight of a lone piebald horse grazing a few hundred yards away. Forty yards away from it, something was lying on the ground.

Mary roused her father, who was due to rise shortly. He dressed and looked out of the window.

'That could be a man lying on the ground,' he said. Accompanied by his ramrod Wes Bailey, whom he called out of the bunkhouse, he hurried towards the object lying on the ground.

When they reached Brad, Bellamy pulled the bloodstained shirt up and took a look at the wound.

'He's still alive,' he said to Bailey, 'but it looks like he's been bleeding pretty bad. Let's carry him to the house. And we'll take the horse as well. Like you can see, it's a Lazy Z horse. We'll put it in the barn for the time being.'

When the two men reached the

house with Brad, Bellamy's wife recognized him, and led the way to a small spare room with a bed inside it. The two men laid Brad on the bed. Mary had followed them in, and Bellamy and his wife exchanged glances as they noticed the look of extreme concern on the face of their daughter as she stood looking down at Brad's motionless body.

'He'll be all right,' said Bellamy. 'The wound don't look all that serious, but he's lost a lot of blood.'

He turned to Bailey as Grace Bellamy, with Mary helping as best she could, removed Brad's vest and shirt, and prepared to clean and bandage the wound.

'You know, Wes,' said Bellamy, 'what this man did for Mary, and you saw his letter saying he was going to the Lazy Z. It looks like he ran into trouble there. I aim to help him as much as I can.

'When you've put the piebald in the barn, I want you to ride into Barlow, and ask Doc Marvin to come out here as soon as he can. Say we're worried about Mary. And don't say anything to anybody about McLaine turning up here. But don't go just yet. Maybe McLaine'll come round soon, and let us know what happened at the Lazy Z. Put the piebald away, then come back here.'

As Bailey left the house, Bellamy rejoined his wife and daughter. They had cleansed the wound as best they could, and were starting to apply a bandage.

'There's a bullet in there,' said Grace Bellamy, 'but I don't think it's done any serious damage. And the bleeding's stopped. But we need to get Doc Marvin here.'

'Is Wes going for him?' Mary asked her father.

'Yes,' said Bellamy. 'He'll be going shortly. And he'll say nothing about McLaine being here.'

Bailey came in just as the bandaging was completed. A few moments later

Brad stirred and opened his eyes. He looked up at the four people standing over him.

'So I made it,' he said weakly. 'I wasn't sure that I could.'

He went on to tell them, haltingly, of all that had happened at the Lazy Z.

When he had finished he struggled up into a sitting position.

'I did wrong to come here,' he said. 'Jordan's bound to have men looking for me, and I don't aim to cause you any trouble. If you can see your way to lending me a horse, I'll be leaving.'

'No!' shouted Mary, looking at her parents.

'You'll do no such thing,' said Grace Bellamy. 'You're hurt bad, and we're sending for Doc Marvin to come out here and see you. There's a bullet in your side that's got to come out.'

'That's right,' said Bellamy. 'Forget about leaving here till you're fit again. And that's final.'

Gratefully, Brad sank back on to the bed.

'Did you see the Lazy Z horse I rode here on?' he asked.

'Right now it's hidden in the barn,' Bellamy replied.

'I tried,' said Brad, 'not to leave any tracks that would help anybody from the Lazy Z to follow me here.'

'That's good,' said Bellamy, 'and I've just had an idea that might send anybody who's looking for you on a wild-goose chase. All it needs is for you, Wes, to get a message to Frank Carver in Barlow.'

He turned to Brad.

'Frank used to work for me till he retired,' he said, 'and we were pretty close. He'll be glad to help. But just now I reckon it's time you took some rest, and Wes needs to be riding off for the doctor.

He left the room with Bailey, and explained what he wanted Frank Carver, in Barlow, to do. Then the ramrod rode off fast, to the south. When he reached Barlow, he called first on the doctor, who said he would set off immediately for the Circle B.

Then Bailey went to a small shack close to the trail leading south out of town. The shack belonged to Frank Carver. Carver was a short man in his late sixties, cheerful despite the rheumatism which plagued him nowadays. He answered the foreman's knock on the door, and let him in.

Bailey explained the situation to Carver, and passed on Bellamy's request for help. Carver didn't hesitate.

'I'll go along to the saloon right now,' he said.

Bailey thanked the old man, then made a further request.

'I'd like to stay in town out of sight for a spell,' he said, 'to see if anybody from the Lazy Z comes to town asking about the man who called himself Ford.'

'You're welcome, Wes,' said Carver. 'I'll come and let you know as soon as anything interesting happens.'

6

Carver walked along to the saloon and went inside. There was no sign of anyone from the Lazy Z in town. He walked up to the bar and asked for a beer. Apart from himself, there were only two customers in the saloon. They were seated at a table close to the bar.

Grundy, the barkeep, handed Carver his beer. He was not a particular friend of Carver, but the two men usually exchanged a few words when Carver was in the saloon.

'You still having trouble with the rheumatics?' asked Grundy.

'I sure as hell am,' Carver replied. 'It was pretty bad last night. I had to get up around dawn. And a funny thing happened. I was wondering if you knew anything about it.'

'What was that?' asked the barkeep, wiping some spilt beer off the bar.

'It was just starting to get light,' said Carver, 'and I was looking out of the window. I saw a rider coming out of town, heading south. He was on a piebald horse, riding real slow-like. He was hunched in the saddle, and swaying a bit. Maybe he was drunk.'

'Did you know the rider?' asked the barkeep.

'I couldn't see him too well,' Carver replied, 'but I'm pretty sure he was a stranger to me. Oh, and one other thing I forgot to mention. He was riding bareback.'

'Can't think who it would be,' said Grundy. 'I can't think of anybody living in town who owns a piebald. And who would be out riding that time of day?'

He looked over towards the swing-doors as they were pushed open. Paxton of the Lazy Z entered the saloon, followed by four of his hands. They walked up to the bar, and the barkeep moved along to stand in front of them.

'We're chasing a horse-thief,' said

Paxton loudly, so that the customers could hear him. 'His name's Ford, and likely he's been injured. He stole a piebald horse from the Lazy Z last night. Has anybody seen him in town?'

Grundy looked across at Carver, then pointed to him. 'From what he's just told me,' he said, 'I reckon that Frank Carver there might have seen him.'

Paxton walked along to stand beside Carver.

'Is that right?' he asked.

'Maybe so,' said Carver. 'Around dawn I saw a rider on a piebald pass my shack, heading south. The way he was riding, he could have been injured. He was on the tall side, and was wearing a Texas hat. And another thing, he was riding bareback. And that's about all I can tell you. I only saw him for a minute or two.'

'That sure sounds like Ford,' said Paxton, and went on to ask Carver a few more questions about the horse and rider, without gaining any further useful information.

'We'll follow him south,' said Paxton to his companions. 'He's got a good start, but I figure that maybe he ain't riding so fast.'

He led his men from the saloon. They all mounted and rode off along the trail leading south from town. Bailey, looking out through the window of Carver's shack, saw them pass. Ten minutes later, Carver joined him.

'Paxton swallowed it, hook, line and sinker,' said Carver. 'I wonder how long it'll be before he and his men give up the chase.'

'A while, I reckon,' said Bailey, 'and it's all thanks to you. When they do give up, I don't see any reason why they would suspect that McLaine's still somewhere around here.'

Bailey left the shack and rode off towards the Circle B. Half-way there he caught up with the doctor in his buggy, and accompanied him for the rest of the way.

When they reached the ranch house, Bellamy took the doctor, a long-standing friend of his, into his confidence. He explained that Brad was the one needing attention, and told him about Brad's pursuit of Jordan, and the reason for it. He also told him Brad's real name. When he had finished, the doctor went in to see Brad.

He took the bandage off, and had a look at the wound.

'There's a bullet needs to be taken out,' he said. 'It won't take me long, but it's going to hurt.'

Five minutes later Brad took a deep breath and relaxed, as Marvin showed him the bullet.

'You're lucky,' said the doctor. 'I don't think there's any serious damage. I reckon it should heal up all right, provided you stay where you are for a while. I'll ride out again tomorrow.'

He applied a new bandage to the wound, then spoke to Brad again.

'I know how you got this bullet,' he said, 'and nobody in town is going to hear from me about you being here.'

'I'm obliged to you,' said Brad.

Marvin took a look at Mary's ankle,

pronounced himself satisfied with her progress, and departed for Barlow.

Bellamy told Brad how Carver had sent Paxton and his men on a wild-goose chase.

'That's good,' said Brad, 'and I'm beholden to your friend. But I know for sure that Jordan's real set on seeing me dead. And when Paxton gets back without finding me, it's just possible that Jordan'll send some Lazy Z hands to nose around here. Which is the last thing we want. Maybe we could stop that happening if your friend in Barlow would help us out again.'

He explained his plan to Bellamy.

'Let's do it,' said the rancher. 'I reckon there's a good chance it'll work. I sure don't want anybody from the Lazy Z poking around here.'

Bellamy called the foreman in to discuss the plan, and when darkness had fallen the foreman went for his own horse, collected the Lazy Z piebald from the barn, and led it in the direction of Barlow. When he was within half a mile of the town he circled it, and approached Carver's shack from the south.

He knocked on the door of the shack, waking the sleeping man inside. He apologized to Carver for disturbing him, then asked the old man if he'd be willing to give some further help to Bellamy.

'Sure,' said Carver. 'I can't tell you how much I enjoyed pulling the wool over Paxton's eyes. What do I do this time?'

Bailey carefully explained the plan of action, and handed Carver the soiled Texas hat he had brought with him. Then they went outside together and put the piebald out of sight in a small enclosure at the rear of the shack. When this had been done Bailey returned to the Circle B.

Three days after this, in the late afternoon, the doctor drove out to the Circle B and checked that both his patients were progressing satisfactorily. He had been told by Bellamy of the latest plan to foil Jordan, and he brought news from Carver of what had happened.

According to the old-timer, Paxton and his party had arrived at Barlow earlier that day, after an unsuccessful search for Ford. Carver had stopped them as they rode past his shack, and he showed them the piebald horse at the rear. He told Paxton that the horse had been left with him just after dawn by a ranch hand from a ranch somewhere south, who was rushing to see a father who was seriously ill somewhere near Amarillo.

Carver told Paxton that the ranch hand had spotted the piebald standing near the north bank of the Red River, which ran some way south of Barlow. There was no sign of its owner, but not far from the horse, at the top of the steep riverbank, he had found a Texas hat. There were signs of blood on the riverbank, and marks indicating that somebody might have fallen down the bank into the water, which was running fast and high at the time.

The ranch hand, Carver told Paxton, had left the horse and hat with him, asking him to return the horse to the Lazy Z, since he had no time to do this himself.

'Carver told me,' said the doctor, 'that he was sure that Paxton had believed his story, and that the search for Brad would now be abandoned.'

'That's good news,' said Brad.

As Brad and Mary convalesced they spent a lot of time together, each feeling strongly attracted to the other. As the time fast approached when Brad would be fit to ride again, he began to plan his next move against Jordan. He decided that if Jordan was still at the Lazy Z, he would make another attempt to capture him during the night, and take him away from the ranch without disturbing Paxton and his men.

Two days later, early in the morning, Doc Marvin arrived. He pronounced Mary fully recovered and Brad fit to take to the saddle. Then, just after midday, Bailey, who had been occupied in the south-west corner of the Circle B range, rode in with some news for Brad.

'I ain't forgotten that description you gave me of Jordan,' he said, 'and I reckon I saw him earlier today.'

He went on to tell Brad and the Bellamys that he had been riding close to the border with the Lazy Z when four riders had passed close by him, in a direction which, if they kept to it, would take them to Amarillo. He had recognized two of them as Harker and Fletcher from the Lazy Z.

The other two had been strangers to him, but he realized that one of them closely fitted Brad's description of Jordan. The fourth rider was very tall and slim. He was dressed in black and Bailey thought he was wearing a pair of six-guns. He had watched the four until they passed out of sight. Then he had raced back to the Circle B with the news.

Brad asked Bailey to describe the man he thought was Jordan.

'That sure sounds like him,' said Brad, when the foreman had finished. 'As for the tall rider, he sounds very much like Wilson, the gunslinger Jordan hired to find me. Maybe Wilson's the man Jordan was waiting for to help him in the operation he was planning. Maybe Wilson has given up the search for me for the time being.

'My guess is that Jordan and the others are on their way to Amarillo to carry out the operation he talked to me about at the Lazy Z. It's a pity I wasn't there long enough to hear the details of what he was aiming to do. I've got to get on his trail right away.'

He got Bailey to give him the location of the point at which the four riders had passed out of his view.

Bellamy offered Brad the loan of a horse, and half an hour later he was ready to leave. He had a few moments alone with Mary before he rode off.

'Will we see you again?' she asked him.

'You can count on it,' smiled Brad.

'I've got to return the horse. But that ain't the only reason. I want to see you again. As soon as I've dealt with Jordan, I aim to hightail it back here.'

'I'll look forward to that,' said Mary, 'and likely I'll offer up a prayer or two that you come to no harm.'

Brad rode to the point at which Jordan and the others had disappeared from Bailey's view.

He found the tracks of four horses, which he reckoned were those of Jordan and his companions. They had stayed on the trail, and he followed the tracks until nightfall, when he stopped and set up camp for the night.

The following day he found that the riders had continued in the same direction, along the trail leading to Amarillo. When he reached a point a little way south of the town three trails merged. Beyond that point he could not separate the tracks from those of other horses which had passed along the trail. But he was reasonably sure that the four men he was following had ridden into Amarillo or some place nearby.

Brad waited outside town until it was dark. Then he rode along the main street until he spotted a US MARSHAL sign. There was a light inside the building to which it was attached. He stopped outside, dismounted, and walked in through the door.

As he had hoped, his old friend Gil Hanson was seated behind the desk in his office. Brad had worked with Hanson for a spell when the latter had been serving as a county sheriff in Kansas, before becoming a federal marshal. And on one occasion, in a shootout with some stagecoach robbers, Brad had saved Hanson's life.

The marshal, alone in his office, looked up as Brad came in. It was a moment before he recognized his old friend. Then, surprised, he rose to his feet, smiling.

'Brad!' he said. 'It's good to see you.'

Then the smile of welcome faded from his face.

'I was mighty sorry to hear about

123

Cliff,' he said. 'I know you two were pretty close. What brings you to Amarillo?'

Brad gave the marshal an account of the events which had taken place since the murder of his brother, ending with his pursuit of Jordan and the others when they left the Lazy Z.

'It looks to me,' he said, 'like they're hiding out somewhere in Amarillo, or near by. And from what Jordan said to me before he found out I was the one who killed his brother, I think he's planning some sort of robbery here.'

'That's quite a story,' said Hanson. 'We've been after Jordan and Wilson for a long time. Maybe there's a chance now of catching them both, as well as the other two. There's plenty of places they can hide in town if they're willing to pay for the privilege, and we could mount a search for them.

'But that could scare them off, and I reckon a better plan would be to try and figure out what their target is, and see if we can catch them in the act.'

'You any idea what that target might be, Gil?' asked Brad. 'You reckon it's likely to be in Amarillo?'

'Jordan's done a few bank robberies in his time, more than any other sort,' said Hanson. 'That's where the big money is. I reckon the most likely target is the bank on the other side of the street, opposite the hotel.'

'If that's the case,' said Brad, 'maybe they'll take a day or two to look the bank over, before the robbery takes place. Jordan would probably send Harker or Fletcher to do that. They ain't so well known as Wilson and himself.'

'I reckon you're right,' said the marshal, 'and the more I think about it, the more I believe that this bank's the likely target. Business is booming in town right now. A raid on the bank, if everything went according to plan, would bring in a rich haul for the robbers.

'I'm going to bring the Texas Rangers in on this. We need to watch the bank for any sign of the gang. And I'll warn the bank manager.'

'Maybe I could watch the bank from the hotel,' suggested Brad, 'provided I can get a room overlooking the street. I'd have no trouble picking out Harker and Fletcher, as well as Jordan. But I'll have to stay out of sight. They think I'm dead, and any sighting of me before the raid would be sure to scare them off.'

'A good idea,' said Hanson. 'I think you're right about them wanting to look the bank over before the robbery. You go to the hotel and see the man who owns it. He's a friend of mine. Say I want you to have a room overlooking the main street. Ask him not to tell anybody about any connection between you and myself. In the morning I'll get one of my deputies to join you in your room. If you spot any of the gang he can bring word to us.

'What I'm going to do myself right now, is to talk with the banker and the ranger captain. I'll tell them of the danger that the bank might be robbed.

We'll work out a plan to deal with Jordan and the others if they do turn up. The deputy'll tell you about it when he sees you in the morning.'

Brad stabled his horse, then went to the hotel. On passing the marshal's request on to the owner, he was given a room overlooking the main street. From it he had a good view of the bank entrance and the alley which ran down one side of the building. At Brad's request the owner said he would arrange for meals to be brought to the room.

Early the following morning Brad was joined in his room by Crane, one of Hanson's deputies. While Brad sat on a chair near the window, and kept a constant watch on the street below, the deputy sat on a chair close by, and chatted with his companion.

They saw Denny, the bank manager, arrive at 9.30 to open the bank; a teller arrived shortly after. Between then and noon, when the bank closed its doors for an hour, there was a regular flow of customers passing in and out, but no sign of Jordan and his gang.

Half an hour after the bank reopened Brad stiffened as he saw Fletcher walking along the boardwalk towards the hotel. There was no sign of any of the other members of the gang.

'It's Fletcher!' he said. 'He's on his own. Let's see what he's up to.'

Fletcher stopped on the boardwalk outside the hotel, directly under the window of Brad's room. Standing with his back to the hotel, he spent some time looking towards the bank across the street. Then he looked up and down the street. Eventually he crossed over and walked along the alley at the side of the bank, to disappear from view.

He reappeared a few minutes later and went into the bank. So far as Brad could see, there were still no other members of the gang in the vicinity.

'I reckon Fletcher's checking the bank out,' said Brad, 'and the chances are, he'll be coming back with the others later.'

Twelve minutes later Fletcher came out of the bank, and stood for a while on the boardwalk, rolling and smoking a cigarette. Then he crossed the street and walked briskly along the boardwalk in the direction from which he had come, until he disappeared from the view of the two men watching him. It turned out later that he had discussed with the manager the possibility of his opening a large account in the near future. This would have given him the opportunity of taking a close look at the inside of the bank.

Brad turned to the deputy.

'You'd better go and tell the marshal what just happened,' he said. 'My own guess is that the gang'll be turning up later today to rob the bank. I'll keep watching from here.'

On getting the news, the marshal immediately contacted Delaney, the ranger captain, who sent four rangers armed with shotguns to the rear door of the bank. This door, normally securely fastened, was opened by Denny, the manager, to admit them.

The manager then went to the front door of the bank. He stood just inside, and intercepted all customers known to him personally as they entered the bank. He told them that there was a possibility of a raid on the bank. He asked them to leave and conduct their business the following day. He asked them to keep to themselves what he had just told them.

A little less than two hours after Fletcher had left the bank Brad saw him again, this time accompanied by Jordan and Wilson. They walked out of the alley alongside the bank and into the main street. They paused for a moment, looking up and down the street, then walked up to the door of the bank. There was no one within sight as they stopped in the doorway to pull up their bandannas to cover the lower parts of their faces. Then they opened the door and stepped inside. There were no customers in the bank. Unknown to Jordan and the others, the stout metal grille which normally ran the full length of the counter had, at the ranger captain's request, been removed before Fletcher's visit earlier in the day.

The teller was standing behind the counter. The manager was seated at a table set well back from the counter and close to a large metal safe standing on the floor. Jordan and Wilson, with guns drawn, ran up to the counter and covered the two men behind it, ordering them to put up their hands. Fletcher turned the sign hanging on the inside of the door, to indicate that the bank was closed. Then he joined the others at the counter.

Telling his two companions to keep the manager and teller covered, Jordan moved to open the door at the end of the counter, which gave access to the other side. But it was securely fastened on the far side. Cursing, he prepared to climb over the counter. Before he could do so the four rangers, each with a loaded shotgun in his hands, suddenly rose up behind the counter.

Simultaneously, the manager and teller flattened themselves on the floor.

Jordan and his partners, completely taken aback to find themselves staring into the barrels of four shotguns, knew it would be suicide to resist. They dropped their weapons on the floor, and raised their hands. Then two of the rangers slipped out of the back door, surprised Harker, who was holding the gang's horses, and captured him without a struggle. All four prisoners were taken to the jailhouse built on to the rear of the ranger captain's office.

Three days after the unsuccessful raid a party of rangers was dispatched to the Lazy Z to arrest Paxton and his men for the imprisonment of Brad and on suspicion of aiding and abetting a gang of criminals. But they were not there. The indications were that they had left hurriedly and had crossed over the border into Indian Territory.

The posse arrived back in Amarillo on the same day that the trial of the four men was held, with Judge Colman presiding.

Jordan and Wilson were already wanted for murders committed by them in the past, and Brad gave evidence concerning the murder of his brother and the attempt by Jordan and his gang to steal a trail herd on the Chisholm Trail. The judge sentenced Jordan and Wilson to death by hanging, this to take place in three days' time, on the expected arrival from Fort Worth of a newly appointed public hangman, Bart Morgan. This would be Morgan's first assignment.

Harker and Fletcher received custodial sentences, and were picked up by a jail wagon on the day following the trial, for transportation to the state penitentiary.

Jordan and Wilson were held together in one cell to await the hanging; in view of their evil and violent reputations they were guarded constantly by an armed ranger who sat in a position which gave him a clear view of the men inside the cell.

Brad was in the US marshal's office when the jail wagon left with Harker and Fletcher. He told Hanson that he intended to stay on in Amarillo until the hanging took place. In the meantime, he had to think seriously about what direction his future life would take now that Jordan had been dealt with by the law. But he had concluded that before making any final decisions he must go and see Mary on the Circle B.

'I can offer you a job as a US deputy marshal,' said Hanson. 'Think about it.'

'I'll do that,' said Brad.

On the evening of the day before the hanging the ranger captain left the office for his house, leaving Ranger Murdoch in charge of the prisoners. Murdoch was an experienced lawman who could be relied on not to offer the slightest chance of escape to the prisoners.

About an hour before midnight Murdoch was sitting outside the cell holding the two prisoners when he heard a loud knocking on the door leading into the office from the street. He rose from the chair and, taking his shotgun with him, he walked through into the office and over to the door, which was securely fastened on the inside. He slid aside a small panel in the upper half of the door, and looked through the aperture.

He could see, in the light from a lamp hanging outside the door, a short, stocky man, with a long grey beard, who was a complete stranger to him.

'Who're you?' he asked, 'and what d'you want? The captain ain't here right now.'

'That's all right,' said the stranger. 'I don't need to see him just now. My name's Morgan. Just got in from Fort Worth. Early tomorrow I aim to hang those two prisoners you've got in there. It'd save me time in the morning if I could take a look at them now. Need to know their height and weight.'

'We've been expecting you,' said Murdoch, 'but I reckon you should see the captain before you come inside.'

'No need to bother him at this hour,' said the man outside, 'but you're right to be careful about who you let in. You need to see proof of my identity.'

He took a folded sheet of paper from his pocket and handed it through the aperture to Murdoch. The ranger unfolded it, and carefully read the statement, signed by the governor, that the bearer, Bart Morgan, was an officially appointed public executioner. Murdoch opened the door and handed the paper back.

'Come in, Mr Morgan,' he said.

He fastened the door before leading the way to the cells. The man behind him, seeing that there was only one guard in the building, produced a long-bladed knife from inside his jacket. Using all his strength he drove it deep into Murdoch's back. The ranger jerked forward, then twisted round in an effort to bring the shotgun to bear on the man behind him. But before he could complete the move he suddenly collapsed and fell to the floor. One leg gave a convulsive kick. Then he lay still. His assailant bent down and picked up the shotgun.

As Murdoch went down, Jordan and Wilson left their bunks and ran to the door of the cell. Jordan recognized the man standing over the guard. It was Mason, an outlaw who had occasionally joined up with the Jordan gang. Jordan wasted no time on preliminaries.

'The cell keys are hanging on the office wall, near the desk,' he said. 'Get us out of here, Mason.'

Without speaking Mason passed the guard's shotgun through the bars to Jordan, then ran into the office for the keys. He returned and unlocked the cell door. The two prisoners came out. Jordan bent down to look at Murdoch, then turned to Mason.

'This man's still breathing,' he said.

'Not for long,' said Mason. 'I know where my knife went in. And it went in hard and deep.'

'All the same,' said Jordan, 'we'll tie him up and gag him, and lock him in the cell.'

When they had done this, using some rope they found in the office, Mason told the others that he had three horses waiting just outside town.

They slipped out of the building and, keeping off the street and in the shadows, made their way to the horses.

'Paxton knew we were in jail and got in touch with you?' asked Jordan.

'That's right,' Mason replied. 'He asked me to help set you free. It was his idea for me to ambush the hangman and take his place. He reckoned I have the look of a hangman about me, which would help me get away with it.'

'Where's the hangman now?' asked Jordan.

'Lying just off the trail, about nine miles south-east of here, with a rifle bullet in his head,' Mason replied. 'I didn't have the time to bury him.'

'We'd better get moving, then,' said Wilson. The three men mounted and rode off in a south-easterly direction.

7

It was six o'clock in the morning when Ranger Trent, Murdoch's relief, knocked on the door of the ranger captain's office. When Murdoch failed to make an appearance Trent tried the door and found it unfastened. On going through to the cells, he found that the prisoners had escaped, leaving Murdoch lying on the floor of the locked cell.

Hurriedly, Trent went for the spare cell key in the office. He entered the cell, and knelt down by Murdoch. He removed the gag and the ropes securing his arms and legs. He saw the blood which had come from the knife wound in the injured man's back, and he could tell that Murdoch was barely alive.

As Murdoch started to speak, haltingly, and in a barely audible voice, Trent bent down further in order to hear what the injured man was saying. Murdoch told him how he had been tricked into letting a stranger inside before being knifed in the back and locked in the cell. He went on to describe the bogus hangman, saying that he had heard Jordan call him Mason. He had barely finished speaking when his head fell sideways, and he was dead.

Trent ran to tell Captain Delaney what had happened. Two hours later a posse of four rangers, accompanied by Brad, rode off in search of Jordan and his two companions. Donovan, the ranger in charge, was an experienced tracker, and he soon found the place, just outside town, where the horses had been picketed recently. The posse followed the tracks of the three horses, which were taking the same trail to the south-east along which Mason had ridden, in the opposite direction, on his way to Amarillo the previous day.

With Donovan in the lead they followed the tracks for nine miles, until

Donovan came to a stop. He motioned to the others to keep back, then dismounted and studied the ground.

'Something happened here,' he called out. 'There's blood on the ground.'

A few minutes later they found the body of the hangman in a patch of brush close to the trail. He had been shot through the head. He was recognized as Bart Morgan by one of the rangers, who had seen him recently in Amarillo.

Leaving one ranger behind to arrange for Morgan's body to be taken to Amarillo, the posse continued to follow the tracks of Jordan and the others. When darkness fell, and they made camp for the night, Brad realized they were only a few miles from the Circle B, and he decided to pay a visit to the Bellamys.

On arriving at the Circle B ranch house he was welcomed by the family, who told him that they had heard of the arrest and trial of Jordan and his gang. They were also aware that Paxton and his men had deserted the Lazy Z. Brad told them of the escape of Jordan and Wilson, engineered by a bogus hangman. Then, before leaving, he had a few minutes alone with Mary.

'I'm set on capturing Jordan again, Mary,' he said, 'but once that's done I aim to make a beeline for the Circle B. It's been on my mind for quite a while that what I really want to do when Jordan's been taken care of, is marry you and settle down to ranching. The question is, are you in favour of the idea?'

She smiled at him.

'The way I've been worrying about you lately,' she said, 'I reckon I must be. You get back here just as soon as you can. I'll be waiting for you.'

Brad returned to the rangers' camp, and on the following day, still following the horse-tracks, they reached the point where the three riders had crossed the border into Indian Territory. There the rangers abandoned the chase, but Donovan told Brad that a message would be sent to the US marshal at Fort Smith, telling him that Jordan and his two companions had crossed into his territory.

Brad took his leave of the rangers, and followed the tracks for a few miles until they angled off the main trail. Shortly after that he lost them, but he judged that they were heading roughly in the direction of Lester, near which town the Jordan gang had been hiding before their attempt to steal the trail herd.

Brad had a feeling that Jordan, now that he and the others were safely out of Texas, might be heading for Lester on a mission of revenge, suspecting that Hart, the saloon-keeper, must have talked to somebody about the plan to steal the herd. Otherwise, how was it that the trail boss and his hands were expecting them?

He thought that his hunch was probably right when, on the following day, he rode into a small settlement and was told that three men answering the descriptions of Jordan and the others had passed through the previous day.

Brad rode on in the direction of Lester. He arrived at the town two days later, not long after daybreak. He rode up to the saloon and dismounted. He could see a CLOSED notice on the door. As he banged on the door he had a premonition that he had arrived too late.

After a short delay the door was opened by Kelly, the barkeep, who recognized Brad from his previous visit. Brad said he wanted to see Hart, and Kelly let him in. Obviously shaken, he told Brad that the saloon-keeper had been found dead that morning in his private room at the saloon.

According to Kelly, Hart had been left alone in the saloon when it closed late the previous evening. Somebody, maybe more than one person, must have entered the saloon during the night, to subject Hart to a severe beating, then to stab him to death.

Kelly said that the undertaker had

collected the body, and messages had been sent to Fort Smith reporting the murder, and to Hart's brother, who lived in Fort Worth.

Brad told Kelly that he was almost certain that the man responsible for Hart's death was an outlaw called Jordan, known both to himself and to Hart. He told how Jordan had murdered Brad's own brother.

'I aim to catch Jordan, and hand him over to the law,' he said. 'D'you mind if I take a look at the room where Hart was killed?'

'Help yourself,' said Kelly. 'When you knocked on the door, I was just thinking I'd better clean up a bit in there. The furniture's been knocked around some, and there's blood on the floor.'

He led the way into Hart's private room and pointed to one of the corners, where Brad could see signs of blood on the floor.

'That's where the body was lying, face down,' said Kelly.

Brad looked round the room, then walked over to the corner, and bent down to look at the floor. It was clear that Hart had bled profusely for a while. Brad was just about to straighten up when something on the floor, close to the bloodstain, caught his eye.

It was dark in the corner, and Brad asked Kelly for a lighted oil-lamp. When the barkeep brought this they both knelt down and, with the help of the lamp, looked closely at the floor around the bloodstain. Scrawled in blood on the floor, presumably by the finger of the dead man dipped in blood, they could just make out the two words JORDAN and PALIMA. The last A in PALIMA was very faint, as though Hart's strength had been fast ebbing away.

'It looks like Hart stayed alive for a short while after the killers had left,' said Brad. 'Maybe he heard them talking about where they were heading when they left here.

'I'm pretty sure that Jordan, with two

other men called Wilson and Mason, have been in this room. I followed them from Amarillo. And like I said, maybe Palima's the place they were heading for when they left here. Does the word Palima mean anything to you?'

Kelly scratched his head and searched his memory for a short while before he replied.

'No,' he said. 'Can't say I've heard the name before.'

'Same here,' said Brad. 'Is there anybody in town who's moved around a bit who might know?'

'Your best bet is Phil Tranter,' said Kelly. 'He's retired now. Used to be a stagecoach driver. Worked for several lines in his time. Let's go and see him.'

They found Tranter in the small house which he occupied along the street. He was a short, bearded man, sprightly for his years. He was quick to answer Brad's question.

'Sure, I know where Palima is,' he said. 'I ain't never been there, but I happen to have a nephew, Tom Tranter, who settled there a while back. I hear from him now and again. He runs the livery stable there. It's about eighty miles south-east of here. Head south-east when you leave here, and you shouldn't have no trouble finding it.'

'I'm obliged for the information,' said Brad, and explained briefly to Tranter the reason for his interest in the location of Palima.

'Maybe Tom can help you,' said Tranter. 'I'll give you a letter for him asking him to do anything he can.'

'I appreciate that,' said Brad. 'If I'm going to catch Jordan I'll need all the help I can get.'

He and Kelly waited while Tranter laboriously scrawled several lines on a sheet of paper. When he had finished he put it in an envelope which he handed to Brad.

A little later, back at the saloon, Brad told Kelly that he would be leaving Lester after taking a meal, followed by a few hours' sleep at the hotel. He asked Kelly to tell any lawmen who turned up who Hart's killer was, and that he himself had gone to Palima, hoping to catch up with Jordan and the others.

'I ain't exactly an expert at following tracks,' said Brad, 'so in order to save time I'm going to take a chance, and head straight for Palima.'

Brad left in the early hours of the morning and reached Palima around noon the following day. It was a small place. There was just a single street, lined with buildings on either side. He rode along the street until he spotted a LIVERY STABLE sign on his right. He rode up to the stable, dismounted, and walked inside. Tom Tranter, the livery-man, walked up to him from the rear of the premises.

'Mr Tranter?' asked Brad.

'That's me,' said the liveryman, a stocky, pleasant-looking man in his fifties.

'I've a letter here from your uncle in Lester,' said Brad, handing the envelope over.

Tranter read the letter a couple of

times, then smiled at Brad.

'I'll help you any way I can,' he said.

Brad told him about his pursuit of Jordan and the reason behind it.

'There's a possibility,' he said, 'that Jordan and the other two men with him are in hiding somewhere around here.'

He described Jordan and the others, and asked Tranter if he had seen any of them in town recently.

'No, I ain't,' said Tranter.

'You got any idea where they might be hiding out around here?' asked Brad.

'Nowhere I can think of,' Tranter replied. 'We ain't got no ravines or caves in the area.'

'If they are around,' said Brad, 'there's a chance that one of them might come into town. I think I'll hang around for a day or two, in case that happens.'

'I've got a spare room in my living-quarters, with a bunk in it,' said Tranter. 'If you'd like to use the room you're welcome to it. It has a window that gives a good view of the street. And you can eat in the living-quarters with me.'

'I'll take you up on that offer,' said Brad, 'and I'm mighty obliged to you.'

During the rest of that day, and over the next two, there was no sign of Jordan and his companions, but on the fourth day Brad, watching through the window of his room, saw Tranter come into view. He was hurrying along the street towards the stable. Minutes later, he knocked on the door and came into Brad's room.

'I've just been in the store down the street,' he said, 'and a man I never saw before came in just as I was leaving. From what you told me, he ain't Jordan, but he could be the man Wilson you told me about. Like you said, he was dressed in black, tall and slim, and wearing two ivory-handled pistols.'

'That sure sounds like Wilson,' said Brad. 'Was he alone?'

'As far as I could see he was alone,' said the liveryman.

'I'll follow him when he leaves,' said

Brad. 'Maybe he'll lead me to Jordan.'

Tranter glanced out of the window, then drew Brad's attention to a man who was tying his horse to a hitching-rail outside the saloon across the street.

'That's the man I saw,' he said.

One glance was sufficient for Brad. 'That's Wilson all right,' he said, 'I'll go and saddle my horse. Then I'll come back here and keep watch until he leaves the saloon.'

Forty minutes later Wilson left the saloon and rode out of town in an easterly direction. Standing inside the stable with Tranter, Brad prepared to follow him.

'I don't know whether or not I'll be back here,' he said. 'I'm obliged for your help.'

The liveryman wished him well, and Brad, carrying a pair of field glasses with him, rode off after Wilson. He took particular care not to be spotted by the outlaw, even though, from the way Wilson was riding, it looked as though he had no suspicion that he might be followed.

The outlaw had covered about thirteen miles when Brad, lying flat on the top of a rise, and watching Wilson through his glasses, saw him leave the trail, and head towards a cluster of buildings a little way south of the trail. When he reached the buildings, which had the appearance of belonging to a small ranch, Wilson disappeared from view.

Closely scanning the surrounding area with his field glasses, Brad could see that there was no chance, during daylight, of getting closer to the buildings without the danger of being spotted. He decided that before investigating the buildings further he would ride back to Palima to make some enquiries about the ranch which appeared to have been Wilson's destination.

Back in Palima, Tranter told Brad that the ranch that Wilson had ridden to was the Box J, a small horse-ranch, owned by a man named Larkin.

'It looks like Jordan and Mason might be hiding out on the Box J with Wilson,' said Brad. 'What do you know about this man Larkin, and the spread he's running?'

'Next to nothing,' Tranter replied. 'He set up there about two years ago, and only very rarely do we see him or any of his hands here. I heard that he gets all his supplies by freight wagon. I don't know where from. And another thing I've heard is that he don't exactly welcome anybody heading for the buildings who has no business there. Any riders doing that are stopped and told that they're trespassing. Then they're ordered to change direction and ride on.'

'It sure looks like this man Larkin has something to hide,' said Brad. 'Have you been near the place yourself?'

'I've ridden by the place just a couple of times,' Tranter replied, 'and I remember wondering why he'd built such a big house, not having any family with him that I know of. And the barn seemed to me to be a whole lot bigger than was needed for a ranch like that.'

'That's all very interesting,' said Brad. 'Maybe the Box J ain't just an ordinary horse ranch. I'm going to find out whether Jordan and Mason are there with Wilson. If I find that they are I'll come back here and get in touch with the law. Could you help me with that?'

'I can,' said Tranter, 'but maybe we'll be lucky. We're expecting two or three deputy US marshals to call here any time now.'

Brad left Palima after nightfall and headed for the Box J. He stopped well short of the ranch buildings and tethered his horse some way off the trail. It was an hour before midnight.

Cautiously, Brad walked towards the ranch buildings. Lights were still showing inside the house, and also in another building which he guessed was the bunkhouse, with a cookshack standing close by. Then, as he drew closer, he could see chinks of light at various points along the sides of a large building which had the appearance of a large barn.

Stealthily, Brad circled the buildings and discovered that a guard had been posted outside the house, and another one outside the barn. At half an hour before midnight he was puzzled to see the shadowy figures of several men leaving the house and walking through a large door into the barn. By midnight the lights in all the buildings had been extinguished, except for one which still showed underneath the door of the barn. Shortly after this he observed what appeared to be the changing of the two guards.

Brad decided that he needed to keep the buildings under observation in daylight, from a position close enough to help him identify Jordan and his two companions if they came into his view.

He returned to his horse and rode to a small grove of trees which he had pin-pointed the previous day. It was well away from the trail and close enough to the buildings to suit his purpose. He tethered his horse well inside the grove and settled down to await the dawn.

When daylight came Brad positioned himself just inside the grove, with a good view of the ranch buildings. As he watched through the field glasses he saw the guards outside the barn and house leave their posts and disappear into the bunkhouse. A few minutes later a man left the bunkhouse and entered the house.

Shortly after this a movement on the roof of the house caught Brad's attention. A man had appeared in view on a small platform which had been constructed on the apex of the roof. The platform was railed-in and roofed over. An ideal observation post, thought Brad, from which, during daylight hours, visitors approaching the ranch buildings from any direction could be spotted.

Forty minutes later six men left the bunkhouse, walked over to the cook-shack and disappeared inside. They reappeared thirty minutes later and dispersed to various points in and around the buildings. None of the six men bore any resemblance to the three men Brad was watching for.

A little over an hour later the barn door opened and Brad turned his glasses on the man who walked out of the barn, then across to the house, and disappeared inside. He was followed at short intervals by eight other men. Brad studied them all through the glasses, but it was not until the last three appeared, close behind each other, and stood talking together a few minutes before moving on, that he was able to identify them as Jordan, Mason and Wilson.

Several times during the day Brad caught sight of the three men as they moved between the house and the barn. He stayed in the grove until darkness fell, then returned to the livery stable in Palima. He found Tranter in the house and told him that Jordan and the others were staying at the Box J.

'You're in luck,' said Tranter. 'Three deputy marshals rode in this afternoon. They're staying at the hotel overnight. The one in charge is called Warren. I told him about you. I'll go and ask him to come over.'

Fifteen minutes later he returned with Warren, a stocky, capable-looking man in his late forties. The liveryman introduced him to Brad.

'We heard from the US marshal in Amarillo that you were in Indian Territory,' said Warren. 'We know that you and your brother were deputy sheriffs in Kansas, where your brother was murdered by Jordan. And we know that a ranger and a hangman were killed when Jordan and Wilson escaped from jail in Amarillo.'

'That's right,' said Brad. He went on to tell Warren that he had seen Jordan, with Wilson and Mason, on the Box J earlier that day, and that they appeared to be staying there, with a number of other men who were obviously not ranch hands.

'My guess is,' said Brad, 'that the Box J is being used mainly as a haven for outlaws, probably nine of them at the present time.'

Warren had listened to Brad with mounting interest.

'So,' he said, when Brad had finished, 'it looks like there are around nine outlaws in hiding at the ranch. You're fairly sure about that?'

'I am,' said Brad.

'There's a chance we can pull off a big haul, then,' said Warren, 'provided we play our cards right. D'you know how many ranch hands there are on the Box J?'

'Around seven, as far as I could tell,' Brad replied. 'I've been thinking about the best way to capture the outlaws, and one thing I'm certain of is that the ranch buildings should be raided during the night, after midnight. When you do go, I'd sure like to go along with you.'

'I was going to ask you to come along,' said Warren. 'The information you've picked up is going to be mighty useful to us. I'll swear you in as a deputy. But I reckon we need more men for the job.'

After a moment's thought, he continued.

'We're due to rendezvous with two more deputies fifteen miles south of here at noon tomorrow,' he said. 'I'll get one of my partners to ride there and bring them straight back here. The job the five of us were aiming to do can wait a while. We'll raid the Box J tomorrow night. Meantime, we'd better make sure that nobody but ourselves knows what we're aiming to do.'

Brad gave Warren information concerning the layout of the ranch buildings on the Box J, and the locations of the two night guards.

'It looked to me as though the guests are staying in rooms inside the barn,' he said, 'and I've got an idea how maybe we can take them without a lot of gunplay. Can we talk about it?'

'Sure,' said Warren, and they spent

the next forty minutes discussing the tactics to be adopted for the forthcoming operation. Then the deputy departed and Brad settled down to await the arrival of the two additional deputy marshals the following day. When they arrived, in the afternoon, Brad and the five deputies got together to discuss the details of the forthcoming operation.

8

The deputies, accompanied by Brad, left Palima after nightfall and headed towards the Box J. At one o'clock in the morning, well past the time at which they expected the guards had been relieved, they halted at a point well short of the buildings. They picketed their horses and advanced on foot. The only light showing came from under the door of the barn.

Brad went on alone and established that two guards had been posted in the same positions as on his previous visit. He returned to the others, who were standing at a point which, had it been daylight, would have been visible to the guards.

'You got the torch ready?' Brad asked one of the deputies. 'I'm holding it in my hand,' the deputy replied.

'Give us fifteen minutes,' said Brad.

'By then we should be close to the guards.'

Brad and Warren, each accompanied by one of the other deputies, moved silently towards the buildings. Eight minutes later Brad and his companion were crouching against the side of the barn, near a front corner. Shortly after this Warren and his partner occupied a similar position against the side of the house.

They did not have long to wait. The deputy holding the tallow-soaked torch ignited it, and the distant flame immediately attracted the attention of both guards. They reacted in the same way. Both men stepped forward a few paces, then stood still, staring intently at the distant flame.

While the attention of the guards was diverted Brad and Warren moved up silently behind them and pistol-whipped them. Both guards, temporarily stunned, fell to the ground. Quickly they were bound and gagged by Brad and Warren and the other two deputies, before being dragged well away from the buildings into the darkness. Warren then went for the two deputies who had been left behind earlier. All six of them assembled outside the bunkhouse.

With guns drawn, and moving as silently as possible, five of the deputies filed into the bunkhouse, leaving one on watch outside. Brad lit a lamp which was standing on a small table, and they could see six men lying on their bunks, all sound asleep. Any arms that were visible were put out of reach and the six men were prodded awake, to face the guns of the five intruders.

'The first man that makes a noise is dead,' said Warren, and one by one the hands were gagged and bound so securely with part of the large supply of rope the deputies had brought with them that it would be impossible for them to free themselves and raise the alarm.

Taking the lamp with them the deputies left the bunkhouse, checked that there was nobody sleeping in the cookshack, and moved on to the house. They entered cautiously, and on the ground floor they found a large dining-room, with kitchen attached, capable of feeding up to a dozen people. There was also a spacious living-room, with comfortable arm-chairs, card-tables, and a variety of reading material.

Upstairs they found three bedrooms. Unknown to them, one was occupied by Larkin, the owner of the ranch, another by his foreman Kilgour. The third was empty. Larkin and Kilgour, both fast asleep when the deputies entered their rooms, received exactly the same treatment as the ranch hands. Each was left in his bedroom.

'One of them must be Larkin,' said Brad. 'Don't know about the other one. We'll find out later.'

The final target was the barn. The six deputies left the house and walked over to the barn door. Brad opened the door and stepped inside, followed by Warren. The other deputies remained outside.

The light from two oil-lamps inside the barn revealed that only half the inside space was being used for its normal purpose.

Investigation by Warren and Brad showed that what looked like sleeping accommodation for Larkin's guests had been constructed inside the barn, in the form of twelve rooms. The doors to these rooms were in a narrow passage, six doors to either side. The passage ran down the centre of the building. All twelve doors were closed.

Brad and Warren left the barn and had a whispered consultation with the other deputies. They all knew that the men they were after were hardened criminals, used to gunplay, who would have no compunction in killing a lawman when cornered. Each of the deputies picked up one of the torches they had brought with them, then four of them waited while Warren and Brad inspected the outside of the barn. There were no windows in the sections of the walls where the rooms were located, but they discovered twelve small grilles, each about nine inches square. Assuming these had been provided for purposes of ventilation, they returned to the others.

The torches which the deputies were now holding were specially designed to be slow-burning, and to produce a cloud of thick, black, evil-smelling smoke. The torches were lit, then Brad and Warren, each holding over the lower part of his face a large piece of cloth moistened with water from a nearby water-trough, walked slowly into the barn and along the passage between the rooms. The smoke from the torches gradually filled the passage. They stayed there as long as they were able, then went outside to breathe in some fresh air. The second pair of deputies followed their example, then the third.

The whole process was repeated, by which time the passage was filled with dense black smoke, and it was clear that it must be seeping round the doors into the rooms. All the torches were dropped on the ground, well away from the barn, then Brad and Warren ran back into the barn and hammered vigorously on all twelve room doors in turn, at the same time shouting 'Fire!'. Then they rejoined the other deputies just outside the barn door.

Inside the rooms the occupants, awakened by the banging and shouting, smelt the smoke. Their first thought was to get outside the barn as quickly as possible. They were aware that any fire inside the barn could quickly turn into an inferno. Some of them left their rooms clad only in their long johns, others hastily donned pants and shirt before leaving. Each of them, as he opened the door of his room, was met by a wall of thick smoke which brought on a violent and uncontrollable fit of coughing. One by one they stumbled towards the door of the barn.

As each man left the barn, coughing and choking, he was met by the deputies, and ordered, at gunpoint, to lie face down on the ground. Then his hands were quickly tied together behind him. Not a single shot had been fired.

Brad brought a lighted lamp from inside the barn. He and Warren turned the prisoners over, one by one, and closely examined their faces. When they had finished Warren turned to Brad.

'Are Jordan and his friends here?' he asked.

'Wilson and Mason are here,' Brad replied, 'but not Jordan. Maybe he's still inside the barn. I guess the smoke's thinned out a bit by now. I'm going to take a look.'

'I'll come with you,' said Warren, and the two deputies went into the barn to look for the outlaw. But a quick search showed that there was nobody left inside, and they rejoined the other deputies.

'I'm sorry Jordan's missing,' said Warren to Brad, 'but all the same, we've done pretty good. You've identified Wilson and Mason, and I recognized the other six prisoners. There's Latimer, and the two other men in his gang.

Then there's the two Millard brothers, and a man called Casson, who works alone. Apart from Casson, they're all wanted for murder, as well as robery. Judge Parker at Fort Smith's going to be mighty pleased to see all eight of them in his court.

'I'm going to arrange for a jail wagon to come and pick up the outlaws. And I've got to figure out what we're going to do with the rest of the men we've got tied up here. It's all going to take some time. What are you aiming to do?'

'Find Jordan and hand him over,' Brad replied. 'But where can he have gone? I can't see Wilson or Mason telling us.'

'You're right,' said Warren, 'but there's somebody who might. I'm thinking of Casson. He's a cardsharp and a confidence trickster, but not a killer. I've arrested him a couple of times before. We'll have a private talk with him. I'll tell him that if he gives us information which helps us to catch Jordan, Judge Parker will hear about it.'

It was mid-morning when Warren and Brad talked with Casson, after separating him from the other prisoners. Warren told him that they knew that Jordan had been at the Box J two days earlier, and they wanted to know where he had gone. He made it clear that if Casson gave information which helped in Jordan's capture, it would be to his advantage.

'I ain't never met Jordan before,' said Casson, 'but I recognized him from some Wanted posters I'd seen. I happened to mention in his hearing that I'd crossed the Red River from Indian Territory to Texas and back five or six times. He said he had some kin who'd just moved to a place in Texas called Columba, not far south of the Red River.

'He asked me what would be the best place to cross the Red to get to Columba. I told him the best place would be Harper's Crossing, which is just about due south of here. He said he was fixing to visit them in a couple of months' time.

'Now in my line of business, particularly when I'm sitting in a poker-game, I'd never get anywhere if I couldn't read a man's mind. I knew he was lying. And when I saw him ride off the next day I was pretty sure he was heading for Columba.'

Brad thanked Casson, and Warren took the prisoner back to the others. Then he returned to Brad.

'I reckon there's a good chance that Casson's right,' he said. 'Are you heading for Columba?'

'I am,' said Brad. 'It's the only lead I've got.'

'Hang on to the deputy badge for now then,' said Warren, 'and consider yourself as a deputy US marshal so long as you're chasing Jordan inside the Indian Territory.'

Brad left shortly after, and two days later, still in Indian Territory, he rode into the mouth of a narrow ravine which lay in his path. At the far end of the ravine he climbed out on to some high ground. Looking over a long stretch of flat ground to the south, he could see the figure of a man, on foot, moving away from him. The man was stumbling and weaving from side to side. As Brad watched, the man fell flat on the ground, struggled to his feet again, took a few more faltering steps, then fell face down on the ground and lay still.

Brad urged his mount on. When he reached the man on the ground he dismounted, knelt down, and turned the man over. The man he was looking down at was wearing cowboy clothing. He was young, probably in his early twenties, slim, and fair-haired. A blood-stained bandage was wound around his head and there was a large bloodstain on his shirt, just above the left hip. Brad took a look at the wounds. The one on the head looked like a bullet graze, running along the side of the head, just above the ear. The wound on the side could have been caused by a passing bullet tearing the flesh.

The man's eyes opened, and he

looked up at Brad.

'Who're you?' he asked, faintly.

'The name's Brad McLaine,' Brad replied. 'How come you're in such a fix?'

'I'm Rod Saxon,' said the wounded man. 'I was ambushed in a gully a few miles back. I saw a horse lying on the ground ahead of me, but no sign of the rider. Then I was hit by two rifle bullets coming from the top of one side of the gully.

'I fell off my horse, and managed to scramble behind a big rock standing near the side of the gully. My horse ran on, taking my rifle with it, and stopped to graze a few hundred yards up the gully.

'I watched out for the rifleman, and spotted him looking down into the gully. I still had my six-gun, and I took a couple of shots at him. I ain't all that good with a six-shooter, but I must have come pretty close, because I saw him jerk back out of sight.'

Saxon was silent for a few moments.

Then he went on to tell Brad that the next he saw of the man who had ambushed him was a little later, when he climbed down the side of the gully, near where Saxon's horse was standing, walked over to it, and rode off on it, to the south.

'There weren't nothing I could do to stop him,' he said. 'I waited a while, then took off after him on foot. His horse was still alive, but it had a broken foreleg, and I had to shoot it. I could see where its foot had gone into a hole in the ground.'

'Where were you heading when you were ambushed?' asked Brad.

'Across the Red,' Saxon replied. 'I aim to visit my parents. They're running a small ranch near a town called Columba in Texas.'

'It so happens,' said Brad, 'that I'm heading there myself. Now let me take a look at those wounds.'

He took off the head bandage, and cleaned the graze, using water from his water-bottle. Then he lifted Saxon's shirt and cleaned the flesh wound in the same way. He took a spare clean shirt from his bedroll, tore it into strips and used it to bandage the head and side.

'You've had two big strokes of luck,' said Brad. 'A few inches to one side, and either of those shots could have put you right out of action. You need to see a doctor. You got any idea where the next town is to the south?'

'I was heading there when you found me,' said Saxon. 'I've been there before. I reckon it's about twelve miles from here. It's called Tyrone.'

'That's where we'll go, then,' said Brad. 'I've got a good strong horse here. You reckon you can ride behind me?'

'Sure,' said Saxon as he rose shakily to his feet.

Brad helped him on to the horse, then mounted it himself and set off in the direction of Tyrone. As they rode along Saxon explained to Brad that he had helped to drive a trail herd along the Chisholm Trail to Kansas. When the herd had been handed over to the buyer, he had headed south to visit his parents, before heading west for the big Texas ranch near San Antonio where he was employed. Brad told Saxon about his search for Jordan, the killer of his brother, and said that he suspected the outlaw might be somewhere near Columba.

They reached the small town of Tyrone an hour before nightfall and stopped at the doctor's house, marked by a sign over the door. Brad helped Saxon down, then banged on the door.

It was opened by Doc Noble, a small, dapper man, who let them in, then examined Saxon's wounds.

'I guess you know how lucky you are,' he said, when he had finished. 'I'll clean the wounds, put a few stitches in your side, and put some clean bandages on.'

'I'm heading south,' said Saxon, 'and I ain't got much time to spare. When d'you reckon I can ride on?'

'Rest up tonight, and all day tomorrow,' said Noble, 'and I guess a

178

short ride the day after, say as far as Dorando, should be all right. That's provided your friend goes along to keep an eye on you.'

Saxon looked at Brad, who hesitated a moment, then nodded his head. He figured that if he stayed with Saxon until they reached his father's ranch, maybe the Saxons could help him to locate Jordan if he was in the area.

'I'll need a horse,' said Saxon.

'Likely you'll get one at the livery stable along the street,' said the doctor.

They thanked the doctor, and walked along the street to the livery stable, where Brad handed in his horse and Saxon bought a horse and saddle for his ride to Columba. Then they took two rooms at the hotel.

The following day, while Saxon rested, Brad made enquiries as to whether Saxon's horse and the man who stole it, had been seen in town. The result was negative.

Early the following day Saxon went to see the doctor, who renewed the bandages. Then he and Brad left on the half-day ride to Dorando.

When they arrived at their destination they took a couple of rooms at the hotel. Saxon, tired after his ride, went up to his room to rest. Brad led the two horses to the livery stable along the street, then went into the store to make a few purchases.

Inside his room, Saxon took off his gunbelt. Before lying down on the bed he walked over to the window and looked down on to the street below. He opened the window for some fresh air, and glanced at a rider coming along the street towards the hotel. As he turned and started to walk back to the bed it suddenly struck him that the horse the man was riding looked familiar.

He turned, and went back to the window. The rider was passing directly underneath it, and a second look at the horse suggested to Saxon that it could well be his. He looked at the rider, and decided he could be the man who had ambushed him and had stolen his horse.

Moving as fast as he could, Saxon left his room and went downstairs and into the street. He was in time to see the rider dismount, tie his horse to a hitching-rail outside the saloon on the other side of the street, and disappear inside.

Saxon walked across to the horse. One look at the scar on its right hindleg confirmed his suspicion that the horse was his. He hesitated for a moment, then turned and walked towards the store. As he reached it, Brad came out of the door. Saxon told him that his stolen horse was standing at a hitching-rail across the street and the man who had ridden it into town was inside the saloon.

'I'm still serving as a deputy marshal,' said Brad. 'I'll arrest him. But just to make sure nobody gets hurt I'll take him when he's alone and off his guard. Let's see where he goes when he comes out of the saloon.'

Brad and Saxon returned to the hotel and kept watch on the saloon from the window of Saxon's room. They did not have long to wait before they saw the man leave the saloon and walk across to the hotel entrance. Quickly, Brad left the room and tiptoed along the passage to the head of the stairs, out of sight of the desk below. He was in time to hear Wogan, the proprietor, speaking to the man who had just entered.

'I'd like a room for the night,' stated the man.

'Sure,' said Wogan. 'If you'll just sign the register. Thanks. That'll be Room 3. Here's the key, Mr Smith.'

'I'm taking my horse to the livery stable,' said Smith, 'but I'll be right back. What I need right now is some sleep. I've had a long day.'

Brad ran back to Saxon's room, where he had a brief conversation with him. Then he pinned on his deputy's badge and hurried down to see Wogan. He explained that he was intending to arrest Smith for attempted murder and the theft of a horse. He asked him if he had a spare key for Room 3.

'Sure,' said Wogan. He picked up a key from a shelf under the desk and handed it to Brad.

'When Smith gets back,' said Brad, 'just act natural-like, and I'll do the rest.'

He went upstairs, and rejoined Saxon. The two of them let themselves into Room 3, locked the door from the inside, and removed the key. Brad stood at the window, watching out for Smith's return, while Saxon sat on the bed.

Six minutes later Brad saw Smith enter the hotel. He and Saxon took up a position where they would be hidden by the door when it was opened. A few minutes later they heard the sound of a key in the lock. As the door opened and Smith stepped into the room Brad moved up behind him and jammed the end of the barrel of his six-gun into the side of Smith's neck. At the same time he pulled Smith's revolver from its holster and handed it to Saxon. Then he ordered Smith to sit on the floor with his back to the wall.

'You're under arrest, Smith,' said Brad, 'if that's your real name. The charges are attempted murder and horse-stealing. The man you robbed and shot is in this room with me. He's identified the horse you've just taken to the stable as belonging to him. And he actually saw you ride off on his horse after you shot him.

'Keep an eye on him, Rod, while I go and make arrangements for him to be guarded till he's picked up. If he shows any signs of getting up, shoot him.'

Brad turned to leave, then paused.

'Before I go,' he said, 'let's try and find out if his name really *is* Smith.'

While Saxon held a gun to the prisoner's head Brad emptied his pockets on to the floor. He returned all the items to Smith's pockets with the exception of a folded sheet of paper, which he unfolded, read, and placed in his own pocket.

'I'll go now,' he said to Saxon. 'I'll be

back as quick as I can. And like I said before, shoot him if he moves.'

Brad found Wogan in the lobby, standing behind the desk. He told him that Smith had been arrested and that he was going to send a message to the US marshal at Fort Smith, asking for the prisoner to be picked up.

'I can't take him in myself,' he explained, 'because I'm on the trail of the leader of an outlaw gang, and I don't want to lose him. Are there any men in town who might be willing to guard him till he's picked up?'

'We've got just the right man here to organize that,' Wogan replied. 'He was a Texas Ranger until he retired a few years ago, and came to live here with his son. I'll go for him now, and bring him up to Room 3. His name's Harley, Ed Harley.'

Fifteen minutes later Wogan returned with Harley and Brad took the ex-ranger into his own room to explain the situation to him.

'Guarding him's no problem,' said

Harley. 'There's a small empty shack close to the house I'm living in. We'll keep him in there, tied up. I can find three men who'll help me to guard him till he's picked up. And don't worry. Knowing the kind of villain Smith is, we'll be watching him mighty close.'

'I'm obliged for your help,' said Brad. 'I'll guard him for the next few hours while you get things organized. Should we take him to the shack now?'

'Might as well,' said Harley. 'Then I'll go and see the men who're going to help me out.'

Before he left with Harley and the prisoner Brad told Saxon that he needed to have a talk with him when he got back.

It was after midnight when Brad returned to the hotel. He knocked on Saxon's door and went in. Saxon was lying on the bed, with a lighted lamp on a table close by. He sat up as Brad came in. Brad took from his pocket the sheet of paper he had taken from Smith earlier. He handed it to Saxon.

'What d'you make of that?' he asked.

Saxon examined the sheet. It carried a telegraph message addressed to: J. SMITH C/O JENKINS HOTEL ELLSWORTH KANSAS. It was dated twelve days earlier. The message read: EXPECTING MEET YOU NEAR COLUMBA TEXAS. CONTACT BARKEEP MILLIGAN ALAMO SALOON COLUMBA ON 20 JULY FOR LOCATION OF MEETING. JORDAN.

Saxon read the message through twice, then looked at Brad.

'You figure the man who sent this is the man you're after?' he asked.

'Maybe it's just a coincidence,' Brad replied, 'but I think not. Jordan and Smith are both criminals. Maybe they're joining up for some reason. D'you reckon you could manage to reach Columba by the twentieth?'

'I'm a lot better now,' Saxon replied. 'I reckon I could manage that.'

'D'you know this barkeep Milligan?' asked Brad.

'I met him in the saloon in Columba a couple of times,' said Saxon. 'A shifty sort of character, I thought. It looks like he's working for Jordan, acting as some sort of go-between.'

'It looks that way,' said Brad. 'We'll leave for Columba at daybreak. But right now, I'll write a telegraph message to the US marshal at Fort Smith, telling him about Smith being held here. Then I'll write out a report we can both sign, giving the reasons for Smith's arrest.

'I'll give them both to Harley before we leave. I'll ask him to have the telegram sent, and to hand the report over when the deputies arrive to pick Smith up. I'll explain in the report why I'm riding on to Columba.'

9

Brad and Rod left Dorando early in the morning. After crossing the Red River they found themselves approaching the town of Columba just before nightfall on the nineteenth of July. Although tired, Rod was well on the way to full recovery, and said he would stay at the hotel in town for a day or so in case there was any way he could help Brad in his search for Jordan. His parents, he told Brad, were not expecting him at any particular time.

'I'm obliged to you,' said Brad, 'but we'd better ride in separately and pretend not to know one another. You ride in now and I'll follow you in half an hour.'

'All right,' said Rod. 'Just how are you aiming to play this?'

'I'm guessing, from that telegraph message,' said Brad, 'that Smith and

189

Milligan ain't ever met before, so I'll go into the saloon tomorrow and pretend that I'm Smith. I'll show Milligan the telegraph message as proof. If I'm lucky, he'll tell me where Jordan is. After I've seen him I'll let you know what happened.'

They rose early the next morning. Pretending to be strangers to one another they shared a table at breakfast in the crowded hotel dining-room. After breakfast Rod went up to his room, while Brad walked to the saloon on the other side of the street and went inside. The saloon was empty, except for a man standing behind the bar. Brad walked up to the bar to face him.

'Mr Milligan?' he asked.

The barkeep, a short, middle-aged man, nodded, and took a close look at Brad.

'That's me,' he said.

'My name's Smith,' said Brad. 'I was asked to contact you about meeting up with a friend of mine.'

He handed the telegraph message to

the barkeep, who read it carefully, then returned it to Brad, without any suspicion that the man he was talking to was an impostor.

'Just now,' said Milligan, 'Jordan and the others are staying in an old log cabin in a ravine ten miles south-east of here.'

He went on to give Brad directions which would help him locate the ravine. He told him that Jordan would be there till noon the following day.

'Jordan said,' Milligan went on, 'that he wanted you to ride out there either today or before noon tomorrow. And that's all I've got to tell you.'

'All right,' said Brad. After thanking the barkeep he returned to the hotel, where he tore the telegraph message into small pieces, and dropped them in a litter bin. Then he went upstairs to see Rod, who listened with interest to Brad's account of his conversation with Milligan.

'Like you said,' Brad remarked, 'Milligan had a real shifty look about him. As for Jordan, it looks like he'll be leaving the ravine around noon tomorrow, so there ain't enough time to get the Texas Rangers here to pick him and the others up. I'm going to ride out towards the ravine during daylight today, but I'll stop short of it, and wait until nightfall.

'Then I'll go in on foot and look the place over. Maybe I can confirm that Jordan's there, and find out how many men he has with him. If there's no chance of me capturing him there I'll follow him and the others when they leave.'

'What you're aiming to do,' said Rod, 'sounds pretty dangerous to me, but I can see you're set on it. Anything I can do to help?'

'Not right now,' Brad replied, 'but thanks for the offer.'

'In that case,' said Rod, 'I'll ride out to visit my parents on the Box S Ranch. The ranch house is about seven miles south-west of here. If you need any help, call on me there.'

Rod departed shortly after, but Brad stayed in Columba until an hour and a half before nightfall before leaving town. He headed south-east, and stopped when he reached a small, flat-topped hill which had been described by Milligan, who had told him that it was a mile and a half short of the ravine.

He waited there until it was dark enough to allow him to continue without the risk of his being spotted from the ravine. He stopped well short of the ravine, picketed his horse and continued on foot. He moved with extreme caution through the darkness, and eventually reached a position at the top of the wall of the ravine from which he could look down into it.

Almost directly beneath him he could see the dim outline of a small building. A chink of light showed from a window. He waited a short while, then moved carefully down the sloping side of the ravine until he reached the bottom. He could now see that the building was a log-cabin.

He moved up the ravine, away from the cabin, and found four horses on a picket-line. He walked back towards the cabin, then circled it. There was no sign of a guard outside. Light was showing at only one window, in the side wall of the cabin, through a large gap in the shutters.

A cautious look through the gap, thought Brad, might confirm that Jordan was one of the men inside. As he moved towards the window he heard the muffled sound of conversation inside the cabin.

As he stepped forward to place his eye against the gap in the shutters Brad's foot came down on a rectangular sheet of canvas, sprinkled with soil which made it invisible in the dark, and held in position by a heavy stone at each corner. A piece of cord, attached to the side of the canvas nearest to the window, disappeared through a hole in the foot of the cabin wall.

Underneath the canvas was a pit,

nine feet deep, with vertical sides. The top of the pit was rectangular, roughly four feet by three feet.

As Brad unwittingly stepped on to it, the canvas sheet fell into the pit, and Brad followed it. The cord running through the wall of the cabin was loosely attached to an iron bar leaning against the inside wall. As the cord was jerked out of the cabin the bar was dislodged and fell on the floor.

The conversation inside the cabin ceased abruptly, and for a moment there was silence. Then the four men inside the cabin picked up their six-guns and, taking a lamp with them, went outside. With Jordan in the lead they approached the pit under the window, but kept well back from the edge.

'We're not sure, but we're guessing there's a man down there,' shouted Jordan. 'What we're going to do is wait a couple of minutes, and if you haven't thrown your weapons out by then, all four of us are going to empty our six-guns down there.'

It would have been suicide for Brad to ignore the call. He threw out his six-gun, shouting that he had no more weapons.

A few minutes later the end of a rope was lowered into the pit, and Brad was ordered to tie it around his body, under the armpits. Then he was slowly hauled up, dragged over the edge of the pit, and deposited on the ground. By the light of the lamp held by one of the men Brad could see that two six-guns were trained on him.

Jordan took hold of the lamp and held it close to Brad's face.

'Well, damn me!' he said. 'If it ain't McLaine. How in tarnation did he manage to trail me here? I've told you three all about this man and the trouble he's caused me. I never figured we'd catch *him* in the trap we set under the window. Let's take him inside.'

Inside the cabin they tied Brad's hands and feet and sat him against the wall. He looked at Jordan's three companions. He did not recognize them. They were, in fact, Kinsman, Loder and Ball, three outlaw acquaintances of Jordan, who had arranged a meeting with them and Smith to discuss the formation of a new gang with him as leader.

Paxton, Jordan's former partner, who had been running the Lazy Z for him in the Texas Panhandle, had decided, when he was forced to abandon the ranch, that he would go his own way. All the Crazy Z ranch hands decided to go with him.

Jordan asked Loder and Ball to go outside and see if there was any sign that Brad had not arrived there alone. They returned thirty minutes later to report that they had found Brad's horse and that all indications were that he was alone. During their absence Kinsman and Jordan continued the meal which had been interrupted by Brad's fall into the trap. Occasionally Jordan glanced at the prisoner, with a look which boded ill for him.

'In the morning,' said Jordan to Kinsman, after the return of Ball and Loder, 'ride to Columba and find out whether Smith showed up. I'm beginning to wonder if it was through Smith that McLaine knew I was here.'

He looked down at Brad.

'I've been thinking about what we do with this man,' he said. 'As well as killing my brother, he brought the law down on me in Amarillo, and I came very close to being hanged. And we've just heard that he helped the law catch Wilson and Mason. It only seems right to me that we should string him up.

'We'll take him with us when we leave for the Texas Panhandle, and find a place to hang him where he ain't likely to be found for a while. We can rough him up a bit before we put the rope around his neck. That's something I'm looking forward to.

The outlaws made no attempt to engage Brad in conversation, and he himself remained silent.

At daybreak, after a hurried breakfast, Kinsman rode off to Columba. When he returned later in the morning Jordan met him outside the cabin. Kinsman told him that a man claiming to be Smith, but fitting Brad's description, had called on Milligan, showing him Jordan's telegraph message to Smith. Milligan had told him where Jordan and the others were located.

'It looks as though Smith might have been picked up by the law,' said Jordan. 'Was McLaine alone when he rode into town?'

'Yes, he was,' Kinsman replied, 'and Milligan said he was alone when he left town later.'

'All right,' said Jordan, 'we'll leave here at noon, like we planned, and we'll get rid of McLaine as soon as we reach a place I have in mind. Then we'll cross the Red into Indian Territory, and head west for the Panhandle.'

When they left the ravine Brad was riding his own horse, led by Ball, and his hands were tied. They headed west.

After they had been riding for two hours they passed close by some grazing cows carrying the Box S brand. Brad realized they must be crossing the range used by Saxon's father. Just visible to the north, he could see a small cluster of buildings.

Seven miles further on they left the well-defined westward trail they were following, and headed for a small grove of trees just visible in the distance. When they reached it, they threaded their way through the trees to the centre of the grove. Jordan selected a suitable tree and the outlaws dismounted close by it. Brad was pulled down from his horse. Jordan walked up to Brad and stood facing him. The outlaw's temper flared.

'I've told you all what this man's done to me,' he said to his companions. 'He's got me pretty riled, and I'm going to feel a bit better if I give him a beating before we string him up. Two of you hold his arms.'

Ball and Loder, both powerful men,

took a firm hold of Brad. Jordan stepped up to the prisoner, and landed a barrage of heavy punches to both sides of his face. When Jordan paused for breath, his victim's face was bruised and bleeding, and one eye was almost closed. Resuming his savage attack, Jordan now concentrated on the ribs and solar plexus. When the second attack was over, Brad, unable to stand, sagged in the arms of the two outlaws.

'That'll do,' said Jordan, breathing heavily. 'I could give him some more of the same, but I don't want to damage him so bad that he don't feel the noose choking the life out of him. Drop him on the ground. There's some things I want to tell him before we string him up.'

The two outlaws released their hold on Brad, who lay flat on the ground for a moment, then sat up. As he looked up at Jordan, the pain in his head and upper body was intense, and blood was streaming down his face.

'What I want to tell you before you

die, McLaine,' said Jordan, 'is that Mason brought me some news from Paxton when he broke us out of jail. It seems that he found out somehow that the Bellamys on the Circle B near Barlow hid you away and fooled us into thinking you were dead. Another thing I found out was that you and the Bellamy girl were pretty close, and you were aiming to go back to the Circle B after you'd captured me. I've seen the Bellamy girl. She's a fine-looking woman. I figured out a way of getting back at her and her parents and I want you to know about it before you die. There ain't no danger of you passing the information on to anybody else.

'It so happens I have a birthday on the twenty-eighth of July, and I'm planning a present for myself that I won't mind sharing with my friends. On that very day, after dark, we're going to pay a visit to the Circle B to kidnap the Bellamy girl. We're all looking forward to a bit of female company while we're hiding out near

Amarillo, planning a big robbery there.

'They won't be expecting to see the Jordan gang in action again so soon. When the job's done we'll hightail it for the Indian Territory, and take the girl with us.'

Brad listened to Jordan's words with extreme anger and concern for Mary. But his face did not betray his feelings.

'Let's get this over with,' said Jordan, disappointed at Brad's apparent lack of emotion.

Brad was lifted to his feet. Kinsman formed a noose on a length of rope and dropped it over Brad's head. Ball and Loder lifted Brad on to his horse, which was standing under a branch of the tree. Holding the end of the rope, Kinsman climbed the tree and edged his way along the branch over Brad's head. He pulled the rope tight, made several turns around the branch, and made the rope off. Then he returned to the ground.

Jordan walked up to Brad's horse, which was being held in position by

Ball. As Jordan slapped the horse hard on the rump with a piece of rope Ball let go. The horse ran on for a short distance into the trees.

Brad was left dangling from the branch above him. The outlaws watched as Brad's feet gave a slight jerk before the suspended body, apart from a slight swinging movement remained motionless. The outlaws mounted their horses, collected Brad's mount, and rode out of the grove.

But their departure was premature. Their victim was not yet finished. Two things had been overlooked by the outlaws. Firstly, they had not bothered to check that Brad's hands were still firmly tied behind his back. During the ride from the ravine, Brad had been working on the rope which tied his hands together. After some time he had managed to loosen it sufficiently to allow him to draw from the inside of his sleeve the same razor-sharp blade which had enabled him, not long ago, to escape from Jordan's ranch.

He gradually sawed through the rope, and by the time they reached the grove he judged that one sharp tug would break it. In the meantime he tried to conceal the partly severed rope between his hands and his back.

Secondly, the drop experienced by his body when the horse bolted from underneath him was not sufficient to ensure a quick death.

With his head lolling to one side, Brad watched the outlaws through half-closed eyes, as they disappeared from view, and the sound of their voices faded away. It took three attempts before the rope holding his hands together, snapped. Then, fighting for breath, he raised his arms to their fullest extent, and was just able to place his hands over the branch above. Desperately, he inched himself upwards until the branch was underneath his armpits. He was breathing more easily now that the pressure of the noose around his neck had eased.

He rested for a short while, then

removed the noose from around his neck, lowered himself from the branch as far as he could, and dropped to the ground. He sat there for a while acutely aware of the pain around his neck and the effects of the savage beating inflicted on him by Jordan. He decided to head for the Box S Ranch, run by Rod's parents, which they had passed earlier in the day.

He rose to his feet and walked slowly and painfully to the edge of the grove. He looked to the west. The four outlaws had passed out of sight. He started back-tracking along the route they had taken from the ravine earlier. He walked slowly but steadily at first, trying to ignore the pain in his head and body, but as the miles dragged by his pace grew slower and slower, and he started to stumble, and weave from side to side.

* * *

Nightfall was approaching as Ellen Saxon was preparing supper in the ranch house on the Box S. She glanced out of the kitchen window to the south-west, and stopped what she was doing. She stared intently at the distant figure of a man, staggering and weaving in her direction.

She called out to her son Rod and his father, in the living-room. They joined her in the kitchen, and she pointed to the approaching figure. As they watched the man fell face down on the ground, struggled to his feet, stumbled forward a few yards, then fell down again.

Rod and his father Zachary quickly left the house and ran towards the man lying face down on the ground. Rod was the first to reach him. He turned Brad over. He caught his breath as he recognized him, saw his bruised and battered face and the rope marks which the noose had left around his neck. At that moment his father arrived.

'This is Brad McLaine,' said Rod, hurriedly. 'He's the man I told you about. The one who helped me after I was ambushed.'

He knelt down beside Brad.

'Brad!' he shouted. 'What in hell happened to you?'

Brad stirred and his eyes opened. He looked up at the two men. Rod repeated his question.

'It's a long story,' said Brad, weakly. 'You've probably guessed that Jordan had a hand in this.'

'The story'll keep,' said Rod. 'Let's get you to the house, and mother'll have a go at tending your wounds.'

The two men supported Brad as he walked slowly towards the house. Ellen Saxon was waiting at the door, and Rod briefly told her who the injured man was.

'You're sure welcome here, Mr McLaine,' she said, as she led him inside and sat him down on a chair. 'I'll get to work on that face and neck right away. You got any other wounds we can't see?'

'I had a few body punches,' said Brad, 'and I'm pretty sore around the ribs, but I don't think there's any serious damage.'

Ellen Saxon led Brad to a small bedroom, where he sat on the bed while she examined his face and neck, then washed the blood away and applied plaster and bandages where necessary. She handed him a clean shirt of her husband's to put on, then they went into the living-room to join Rod and his father.

Brad told his audience of the events that had taken place since he had parted from Rod in Columba.

'The most important thing now,' he said, 'is for me to get to the Bellamy ranch in the Texas Panhandle just as soon as I can. I've got to warn Mary and her folks about Jordan's plan to kidnap her. And on the way there I'll send a message to the US marshal in Amarillo, telling him that the new Jordan gang's planning a robbery in Amarillo, as well as the kidnapping of Mary.'

'After that beating you had, you really need to rest up here a few days,' said Ellen Saxon.

'I'll be all right,' said Brad. 'I can't afford to wait. I'll set off in the morning.'

'In that case,' said Zachary Saxon, 'I reckon your best plan would be to get on the westbound stagecoach at a way station north-west of here tomorrow morning. Rod can take you there on the buckboard. That way, you'll reach the Panhandle well before the Jordan gang.'

'That's what I'll do,' said Brad, 'and thanks for all your help.'

10

On the following morning Brad felt a little better, and the swelling around his eye was going down. Rod took him to the way station on the buckboard. Brad bade Rod farewell as the westbound stage rolled in on time. A brief stay was scheduled at the way station, during which time the passengers left the coach.

Brad checked with the driver that he could take a spare seat inside the coach. When it was ready to move off he was the last to enter. Apart from himself there were three women and a man inside the coach. They all glanced curiously at Brad's battered face as he climbed in. All of them were heading for Amarillo in the Texas Panhandle.

Two of the women were a mother and daughter called Lane, returning from a visit to relatives in Arkansas. The other woman was a singer, Dolly de Vere, travelling to fulfil an engagement at a theatre in Amarillo. The man was a drummer called Jackson, who was peddling whiskey.

About half-way to Amarillo there was a change of stagecoach, and Brad knew it would still be a day and a half before he reached the point on the route at which he had decided to leave the coach and ride on to the Bellamys at the Circle B. This point was a small town called Lundy, south-east of Amarillo.

Shortly after a change of horses, and still with ten miles to go before reaching Lundy, Brad was dozing in his seat when he heard the driver yelling above him and cracking his whip. As the coach gained speed and he heard the sound of gunfire Brad stood up and looked out of a window. A rider, with a pistol in one hand, was approaching the coach from behind, and slowly gaining on it.

Brad crossed to the other side of the

coach and looked out of the window. Two more riders, also holding pistols, were pursuing the coach. As Brad watched two bullets in succession ricocheted off the side of the coach.

'Everybody down!' he shouted. 'As low as you can get.'

As they scrambled to obey him, Brad lifted his long-barrelled Colt .45 Peacemaker from its holster. It was a more accurate weapon than the more common short-barrelled version. He steadied himself as much as the jolting of the coach would allow, took careful aim at the nearest rider, and fired.

His first shot brought the rider down from the saddle, to lie, motionless, on the ground. He turned his gun on the man's companion. His first shot was a near miss, but the next one drilled into the second rider's chest, and he also fell to the ground. Brad crossed to the other side of the coach.

He saw the third rider, fairly close now, fire a shot in the direction of the driver. Then, seeing Brad, he fired a quick shot in his direction. The shot slammed into the woodwork close to Brad's head. Once again, taking careful aim, Brad fired, and the third rider went down. As he did so, Brad saw the stagecoach driver fall down from his box to the ground. The coach veered off the road.

Brad opened the door and climbed up the side of the coach on to the driver's box. He leaned forward to catch hold of the brake-lever, and pulled hard on it. The brake-shoes gripped and the coach began to slow down. Then, as one front wheel suddenly rode over a rock jutting from the ground, the coach lurched violently and Brad was thrown from the driver's box to the ground.

For a moment it was touch and go whether the coach would remain upright. Then it slammed down again on all four wheels. Losing speed, it came to a halt sixty yards on. Brad had landed awkwardly. He completely lost his balance and, as he fell, his head collided forcibly with a boulder lying on the ground. Stunned, he lay motionless.

Shaken, the occupants of the coach climbed out. Seeing Brad lying on the ground, they ran up to him. Beyond Brad they could see the driver and the three men who had tried to hold up the coach.

Mrs Lane knelt down by Brad's side. She looked him over, then examined the deep, fresh cut on his temple.

'He's breathing,' she said, 'but it looks like he's been stunned by a knock on the head. There's no sign of a bullet wound. Likely he'll be coming round soon.'

'I'll go and see if I can help the driver,' said the drummer. 'I can see that he's moving.'

The women watched as he reached Forrest, the driver, helped him to his feet, and supported him as they walked slowly back towards Brad and the others. The driver was holding his hand to his shoulder, and was limping badly. When they reached the others the driver looked down at Brad.

'He was stunned when he was thrown off the driver's box,' said Mrs Lane. 'How about you?'

'I've got a bullet in my shoulder,' Forrest replied, 'and I twisted my leg when I fell off the coach.'

He looked down at Brad again, then at the three distant motionless figures lying on the ground, and their mounts, which had come to a halt near by.

'Was it Mr McLaine here who shot down those three robbers?' he asked.

'That's right,' replied Jackson. 'That was some shooting, I can tell you. Then he climbed up on the box and slowed the coach down, before he fell off.'

'We owe this man a lot,' said Mrs Lane.

Brad's head moved, and a moment later his eyes opened. His hand went to the wound on his temple, and he sat up. His head was throbbing with pain. He looked up at the people standing over him, then at the stationary coach standing a short distance away. He hesitated before he spoke.

'Maybe you'll find this hard to believe, folks,' he said, 'but I ain't got no idea who you are, and how I come to be here. The last thing I remember is being held prisoner in a ravine near Columba by a band of outlaws. Where are we now?'

'Near a place called Lundy,' said the driver, 'not far from Amarillo. You sure done us a good turn. You downed the three robbers who were chasing us, and you stopped the coach with these passengers inside it after I'd fallen off and the horses bolted.'

'I don't remember any of that,' said Brad, 'and I've got no idea why I happened to be on this coach.'

'You said nothing to us, said Mrs Lane, 'about where you were going, and why.'

'You told me,' said the driver, 'that you were getting off the stagecoach at Lundy.'

'I had two men fighting over me once,' said Dolly de Vere, 'and one of them hit the other over the head with a

217

whiskey bottle. The man who was hit was out cold for a while, and when he came to, he couldn't remember what had happened to him recently. But in a few days it all came back to him.'

The driver spoke to the women.

'There's some bandages and stuff in the coach,' he said, 'and some water. Let's walk on to the coach, and maybe you ladies'll clean and bandage our wounds. I'll get Doc Young in Lundy to take the bullet out when we get there.'

When the women had cleaned and bandaged the wounds on the two men the driver discussed the situation with Brad.

'I've got a bad shoulder and leg,' he said, 'but I'm going to try and drive the coach on to Lundy.'

'No need for that,' said Brad. 'I'm no expert, but I've driven a team or two in my time. I'll drive the coach on to Lundy. You can travel inside. But before we leave, I'll take a look at those three robbers.'

Brad and the drummer helped

Forrest into the coach. The drummer stayed inside, and the three ladies climbed in. Then Brad drove the coach close to the three men lying on the ground. Still suffering from a severe headache, Brad climbed down from the coach. He drew his Peacemaker and approached and checked each of the three robbers in turn. As he reached the last one the man made a feeble effort to rise and pick up the six-gun lying on the ground beside him. Before he could do so, he slumped back to the ground, and died a moment later. Brad returned to the coach.

'They're all dead,' he said to the people inside. 'I guess we can get somebody in Lundy to come out here and pick them up.'

When they reached Lundy they reported the robbery attempt to Hoffman, the agent for the stagecoach line, and the three women and the drummer went to the hotel to await the arrival of a new driver. Forrest and Brad went to the doctor's house.

Doc Young attended to the driver first. The bullet in the back of the shoulder was not deeply embedded, and was soon removed. The wound was then cleaned and bandaged. The leg was then examined.

'No bones broken,' said the doctor, 'but it's badly wrenched. It needs plenty of rest.'

He turned his attention on Brad, who told him of his memory loss and severe headache.

'It seems I fell off the coach and hit my head on a boulder,' he said.

'Were you unconscious for more than a few minutes?' asked the doctor.

'Yes, I was,' replied Brad, 'according to what the other passengers told me.'

The doctor examined the gash on Brad's temple, then noticed the other marks on the neck and face. He asked Brad how he had come by them.

'I just don't remember,' said Brad.

The doctor attended to Brad's head wound before discussing his memory loss.

'I can't tell you,' he said, 'when your memory's likely to come back. But I *can* tell you that the quickest way to get it back is for you to take a spell of complete rest in bed. Take a room at the hotel. I'll have a word with the hotel owner and ask him to have your meals taken to your room. I'll call there tomorrow to see how you're getting on.'

He turned to Forrest.

'Until you're fit to travel,' he said, 'I've got a room here you can use. I want to make sure that bullet wound isn't infected.'

Following the doctor's advice Brad took a room at the hotel. At the back of his mind there was a faint niggling feeling that there was some urgent matter that needed his attention.

Early the following morning his fellow passengers in the coach came to his room to see Brad and wish him well, before continuing their journey to Amarillo.

They were followed by Hoffman, the agent for the stagecoach line. Hoffman thanked Brad for foiling the robbery attempt, and offered him any help he might need.

'You'll be interested to hear,' he said, 'that I took a look at the three dead robbers, and identified them as the Holness gang. They've been robbing coaches in Colorado and the Texas Panhandle over the past three years.'

Brad's severe headache had eased a little overnight, and he spent most of the following forty-eight hours asleep. When he woke on the morning after his third night at the hotel his headache had disappeared and his head felt clearer than it had done for the last few days.

As he stretched, before leaving his bed, he suddenly realized that his memory had returned. Immediately the gravity of the situation hit him. He dressed hurriedly and ran down the stairs to the lobby. Larsen, the hotel owner, was standing near the desk. Brad asked him what the date was. Larsen moved up to the desk, and glanced at the register.

'Today's the twenty-seventh of July,' he said.

'Where will I find Hoffman?' asked Brad, realizing that on the following day there was every likelihood that Jordan and his men would be turning up at the Circle B to kidnap Mary. 'I need to see him urgently.'

'Turn left out of the door,' said Larsen, 'and his office is in the third building on the left.'

Finding Hoffman in his office, Brad quickly explained his urgent need to get to the Circle B as quickly as possible. Hoffman told him that the Circle B was roughly thirty miles away. Brad asked him where he could get a horse to take him out there.

'That's easy,' said Hoffman. 'You can take mine. It's the best saddle-horse around here. I'll be glad to loan it to you.'

'Thanks,' said Brad. 'The other thing I want to do is get an urgent message to Marshal Gil Hanson in Amarillo, or to

Ranger Captain Delaney, if Hanson ain't there.'

'Write the message down, and I'll get a rider to take it,' said Hoffman. 'It should get there early this afternoon.'

Brad wrote the message down and handed it to Hoffman. In it he told of the intention of Jordan and the three men with him to visit the Circle B the following day, with the object of kidnapping Mary Bellamy. He requested that a party of rangers join him at the Circle B as soon as possible.

Brad reached the Circle B around two o'clock in the afternoon. Grace Bellamy saw him through the window as he approached the house. She called out to Mary, busy in the kitchen. Mary ran out of the house to meet him. As he dismounted she looked with concern at the bandage around his temple, and the other faint marks on his face.

'I've been worried that you were in real trouble somewhere,' she said. 'Is it all over now?'

'Not quite,' replied Brad, 'but it won't be long now. And I won't have to leave you again.'

At that moment Mary's father came out of the barn, and the three of them went into the house to join Grace Bellamy. Brad told them about the probable impending visit of Jordan and his men the following day, and his call to Marshal Hanson in Amarillo for help. He said he expected that they would turn up after dark.

'I'll stay here in the living-room tonight,' he said, 'and I'll let the rangers in when they come. I'm not sure when Jordan and the others'll be turning up tomorrow, but I reckon it'll be after dark. When the rangers do get here, we'll get together with them, and decide on a plan to capture those four killers without any of us getting hurt. I've got a few ideas on the subject myself.'

In the evening, after Mary's parents had gone upstairs, she had some time alone with Brad.

'Can I take it,' asked Brad, 'that

you're all in favour of us getting hitched as soon as we've taken care of the Jordan gang?'

'One hundred per cent,' Mary replied, 'and the sooner, the better.'

'You just made me a very happy man,' said Brad. 'I have a bit of money put by, and I've got a hankering to start a horse ranch somewhere, where I can breed quarter horses. But it all depends on whether you like the idea.'

'I like horses,' said Mary, 'and your idea sounds just fine to me.'

Mary went up to bed and Brad settled down to wait for the rangers. They knocked on the door an hour before dawn, and Brad let them in. There were three of them. The one in charge was Donovan who, with Brad in the posse, had pursued Jordan on a previous occasion.

Hearing the arrival of the rangers, the Bellamys came down, and the women prepared breakfast. The foreman and the two hands, who were all aware of the situation, were called in, and during breakfast Brad explained to the rangers how he had learnt of Jordan's plans to kidnap Mary and carry out a robbery in Amarillo.

After the meal they all settled down to discuss a plan to deal with the Jordan gang when they arrived. Brad put forward his ideas and, with a few slight modifications, they were approved.

The two hands were sent outside to keep a constant watch, between them, for riders approaching the ranch buildings from any direction. Brad and the rangers had decided to stay in the house all day. With the help of the foreman Brad removed from its hinges the door to a small unused room upstairs. He left it in the passage outside the bedrooms.

There was no sign of approaching riders during the day, and after nightfall everybody assembled inside the house. The outside door of the house was fastened, and the ground floor windows were covered over on the inside.

At ten o'clock the Bellamys went up

to their bedrooms and all lamps were extinguished in the house. The front door was unfastened, but was left closed. Then Brad, with Donovan, the foreman and two hands went upstairs and stood in the passage outside the bedrooms. The other two rangers stayed in the living-room. Brad and Donovan kept watch through a window which gave a good view of the front door of the house, down below. The window was slightly open.

The Jordan gang arrived on the scene half an hour before midnight. After establishing that there was nobody in the bunkhouse, barn, or other smaller buildings, they approached the house.

Brad and Donovan saw the shadowy outlines of the four men as they approached the house. Donovan tip-toed downstairs, and he and the other two rangers went into a small store-room in the corner of the living-room. They closed the door behind them and locked it. Upstairs, Brad took hold of the handle fitted temporarily to the centre of the door that he and the foreman had removed earlier in the day. He held it upright across the top of the stairs, where it would give the impression of a door fitted permanently in that position.

Moments later the door downstairs was pushed open and the four men came into the house. They lit an oil-lamp standing on a table and looked around the ground floor of the house. Seeing the storeroom in the corner, they tried to push the door open, without success, then moved on. All four approached the foot of the stairs, carrying the lamp with them and holding six-guns in their hands.

Brad, peering around the edge of the door, saw them coming up the stairs, bunched closely together. As the first one climbed on to the top step and reached for the door-handle, Brad pushed the door forward and downward with all his strength, stepping down the stairs as he did so, and holding tightly on to the handrail with his free hand. At the same time he yelled out to the rangers below.

Donovan turned up the wick on the lamp he was holding. He led the way into the living-room, and over to the foot of the stairs. On the staircase, there was complete confusion. All four outlaws lost their balance and fell down the stairs with the door on top of them.

They lost hold of their guns, and Jordan also dropped the lamp he was carrying. Oil spilt on to his clothing, which caught fire. The two hands appeared on the stairs, each carrying a lighted lamp, and Brad and the rangers had no difficulty in taking all four intruders prisoner. The flame on Jordan's clothing was dowsed, using a bucket of water from the kitchen. On seeing Brad the prisoners stared at him in disbelief. They had been certain that they had left a dead man swinging from that tree in the middle of the grove.

The prisoners were taken to the barn, where two rangers would guard them until a jail wagon arrived. Mary and her mother busied themselves in clearing up the mess on the stairs and in the living-room.

'That was a first-rate plan of yours,' said Donovan to Brad. 'When they told me in Amarillo that our job here was to capture the Jordan gang, I never figured it would be so easy.'

The four members of the Jordan gang were tried in Amarillo for robbery and murder. All were found guilty, and were sentenced to be hanged. The sentence was carried out the following day.

Two weeks after the hangings, Brad and Mary were married, and two months later they found just the place they were searching for — a small ranch that was for sale, fifty miles south of the Circle B. They moved in three weeks later.

RAOUL'S TREASURE

Skeeter Dodds

Arriving in Bradley Creek, Jack Strother defends an old man and is pitched into a confrontation with Ben Bradley, the region's biggest rancher. Now an enemy of Bradley, Strother leaves town, but is forced to return on learning that the old man is dying and wishes to pass on something. But what he gives Strother leads him to a mountain of trouble near the Mexican border. Will the future be no more than a grave in the desert?

CHEYENNE GALLOWS

Tyler Hatch

Digging gold in Sonora they had outsmarted the claim-jumpers. Now they aimed to buy the biggest Texan horse ranch this side of the Great Divide. But they stopped at Buck-eye, and Nolan met Abby Lightfoot — half-blooded Sioux, and full-blooded woman . . . Then the big trouble started. It would end hundreds of miles north, where Custer's shadow still lurked and hatred for the white man was part of life. Guns had started the feud and guns would finish it.